LAST CHANCE GULCH

MCCAIN CRONICLES

BOOK TWO

B.N. RUNDELL

WOLFPACK PUBLISHING
PUBLISHING
— EST 2013 —

Last Chance Gulch
Paperback Edition
Copyright © 2023 B.N. Rundell

Wolfpack Publishing
9850 S. Maryland Parkway, Suite A-5 #323
Las Vegas, Nevada 89183

wolfpackpublishing.com

Paperback ISBN 978-1-63977-808-9
eBook ISBN 978-1-63977-809-6
LCCN 2023932619

DEDICATION

To hard work—yes, this book is dedicated to hard work and the satisfaction it brings whether in monetary reward or simple satisfaction. I recently heard about new AI programs that will do all the writing for the operator, taking a simple command and expounding on it in the manner and style dictated. Now, that's not hard work. Where's the sweat and frustration and reward? There is none. And any writer that's worth their salt will tell you that writing is hard work. First there's the thought, then the research, then the painstaking day-by-day pouring out the words to form the end product—a letter, a poem, an article, or a book. There have been times that I have risen from the keyboard, exhausted, both physically and mentally. So, I dedicate this book to the hard work it took to bring it about. And not just by me, but by the proofreaders, editors, cover designers, marketing team, and so many more. Yes, it takes a lot of hard work to get to the place where you can hold this in your hands. And no, there was absolutely *no assistance from any AI program!*

LAST CHANCE GULCH

CHAPTER 1

ROCKSLIDE

The muted underground blast that lifted the shoulder of the mountain, launched the big red dun stallion and his rider off the trail. When the startled horse landed, his head dropped between his front feet and his rear hocks stretched out to the lone cloud in the otherwise blue sky. Elijah McCain was just as shocked as his horse, but he grabbed the saddle horn, drove his feet deep in the stirrups, clutched the leather of the saddle seat with his thighs and rump and pulled hard on the reins, trying to bring Rusty's head away from his feet. The big claybank stallion was determined to show his fury at the unholy blast that lifted dirt, rocks, stumps, and trees and sent them all flying toward the bottom of the arroyo.

The big stallion twisted in the middle, kicked at the clouds, and drove his front feet into the dirt. Eli dug his heels into the ribs of the stallion, hollered at his best four-legged friend, "What's the matter with you, Rusty! You've been through thunderstorms worse'n this! Will you quit! You're gonna be the death of both of us!" He hauled back on the reins, fighting to bring the stallion's head up and keep them on the semblance of trail that hugged the steep mountainside. If he bucked too far to the left, they both would tumble down about two hundred feet of steep hillside before the bottom of the arroyo caught their remains.

The dapple-grey packhorse had been on free rein, faithfully following his longtime stable mate, the clay-bank stallion. The explosion and man-made earthquake had also frightened the grey gelding and the two horses appeared to be competing with one another as to who would be the first to kick a hole in the blue canopy of sky. With snorts, grunts, and the clatter of hooves, the two horses covered almost a half-mile of trail before they began to realize the explosion and eruption were behind them and the only noise and ruckus to be heard was of their own making.

Eli had kept his seat in the double rigged saddle, although his bedroll was somewhere back on the trail and the saddlebags had been rearranged. As Rusty began to slow, and his steps were carefully chosen, Eli succeeded in pulling the lathered stallion to a stop and the grey walked up alongside, both horses trembling and sniffing at one another and looking all about them. Eli sat easy in the saddle, shaking his head and catching his breath as he, too, scanned the hillsides. There was nothing to indicate the presence of a mine shaft, but the blast had come from underground. He guessed the shaft, if there was one, was on the far side of the hill or some-place unseen from where he sat. Wherever it was, and whoever set off that charge, did not know much about the power of explosives and had definitely put too much in the charge.

The cloud of dust rose from the rockslide that

covered the trail behind them and he saw the dust-covered figures of two men come from over the shoulder of the hill and start climbing up the pile of rocks and debris. They paid no attention to Eli until he reined around and started back on the trail to find his bedroll and the change of clothes that was wrapped in the blankets.

The skittish dun sidestepped and trotted as Eli pointed him back toward the rockslide, kicking out at imagined obstacles, when he crow-hopped and almost unseated Eli, just as a bullet whiffed by Eli's ear. He heard the blast of a rifle and dove from his saddle, grabbing his Winchester from the scabbard as he cleared the leather. He dropped behind one of the many displaced boulders, jacking a round in the chamber as he hit the dirt. Another bullet spanged off the rock, chipping a piece off and spiraling across the arroyo.

Eli hunkered down, knowing he was slightly exposed and if the shooter was very good, he was still in danger of taking a piece of lead and the only possible target would be his rump. He tried to make himself smaller just as the rifle boomed again and another bullet whistled overhead. Eli inched to the side, trying to find exactly where the shooter was hiding, and when another shot kicked up dust in front of his boulder, Eli spotted the smoke and sent three quick shots at the scraggly cedar that was the man's cover. He heard a yelp as one of his bullets split one of the branches, sending splinters of bark into the man's face. Eli quickly rolled away from the boulder and put his long legs to work climbing up the steep hillside, dodging behind boulders, stumps, and piñon trees. He dove behind a cluster of rocks as he heard the shooter firing repeatedly, but he saw the man was still targeting the first boulder where Eli had taken his first cover. Eli grinned, nodding to himself, and looking at the rugged hillside, mentally mapping out his route to get above and behind the shooter.

Eli waited until another flurry of shots came from the sniper and he quickly took to the plotted route, still ducking behind any offered cover and moving as quickly and silently as possible. The steep climb was robbing him of his breath, but that was the least of his concern. With quick glances at the shooter's position, he moved above the man, beginning to circle behind him when he stepped on a loose rock that spilled him on his belly. The rock tumbled down the hill, causing the shooter to look high up just in time to see Eli scamper behind another cluster of scrub oak brush and rocks. But no more shots came from the shooter, and Eli crawled forward, searching for a spot that would allow him to get a glimpse of the man below him.

Eli lay still, catching his breath, listening, but the only sound was the low whisper of wind scurrying across the brushy hillside and rattling the skimpy branches. And still he waited. Nothing. The breeze shifted, coming from below and stretching to the hilltop, carrying the low conversation of two men. Random words were discernible by Eli, "Whar? I cain't see nuthin'!" And what sounded like a grunt, the rustling of branches, and the metallic jacking of a lever-action rifle. Eli craned around the low edge of the brush, saw two men, hunkered together, still behind the scraggly cedar tree, both twisting and craning trying to see where their target had gone.

Eli grinned, slowly crawled to the far edge of the scrub oak brush cluster, and quietly rose, watching the two men arguing and trying vainly to find their target. He was only about thirty yards above them, but the rocks and rubble from the explosion offered him ample cover. He lifted his Winchester, aiming it at the two men, and hollered, "Drop your rifle 'fore I kill you both!"

The two men froze, glancing to one another and the man in the tattered felt hat and holding the only rifle, slowly turned to look up the hill. He spotted Eli, mumbled something to his partner, and answered Eli, "Alright, aw'right, I'm droppin' it, just don't shoot!"

"Easy now, lay the rifle down, keep your hands clear of any other weapon, and stand. Face downhill when you're on your feet!" ordered Eli, still holding the sights of his Winchester on the two men. He watched as the two slowly rose to their feet, but the man with the rifle held tight to his weapon. Eli muttered to himself, "Stupid idjits!" He dropped the hammer on his Winchester, that bucked and spat the .44 caliber bullet. The shot cut flesh on the man's arm, splintered the stock, and knocked the rifle from his hands. The shooter screamed, grabbing at his arm, and glared at Eli.

The two men stood, facing downhill, one with arms lifted, the other still holding his arm, shaking his head and mumbling and whining. Eli started downhill toward the men, picking his steps but watching the men closely. As he neared, he asked, "What in thunder are you two doing? You could'a killed me and my horses! Don't you have 'nuff sense to warn somebody 'fore you try blowin' up your little corner of the world!" he paused in his ramblings as he neared the two scruffy looking prospectors, "I oughta just shoot the two of you and put you outta ever'body's misery! Can you give me any reason not to?" he growled as he came closer. "And then shooting at me! You never saw me before, so why were you shooting at me?"

"Uh, uh, we thought you was one o' them claim

jumpers! We'se just protectin' our claim. An' you the one what's trespassin'! We got ever' right to protect our claim!" growled the wounded man, still fussing and squirming, obviously in pain.

Elijah McCain was usually a mild-tempered man, but he had been on the trail since daylight and had allowed his mind to wander, which he knew was a dangerous thing to do, and when the big-shouldered hill burped and blew, he was as angry at the prospectors and his horse as he was at himself. He growled and grumbled as he ordered the two men to walk to the trail ahead of him, "I've gotta get my gear."

He ordered the two to sit at the edge of the trail on a jagged boulder, "An' you!" talking to the one that did none of the shooting, "take care of your partner, while I get my gear together."

A grunt was all that came from the man as he turned to look at his partner's wound. Eli leaned the rifle against a boulder and began picking up his gear, snatching glances at the two men as he moved about. "And don't try anything, I've got a Colt here that I can get to before you move even a step!" He shook the dust out of the blankets, spread them out on the ground, folded them in half and after shaking and folding his other items of clothing and such, rolled up his bedroll and tied it down behind the cantle of his saddle. He turned to look at the two men who sat silent as they watched this stranger fussing and fuming, and asked, "Well? What do you have to say for yourselves?" growled Eli.

"Uh, what'chu doin' here anyhow?" asked the shorter of the two men, the one with the wound. He stood to face Eli; his arm now bandaged by a dirty neckerchief that his partner dragged from his hind pocket. He jammed his thumbs behind his galluses, chewing on a mouthful of tobacco that dribbled down his beard, his corncob pipe, obviously empty, bouncing with his words. The brim at the front was pinned up to the crown of the raggedy hat, giving him the appearance of someone that ran into a wall and smashed his nose, chin, and hat brim. Trying hard to look mean and tough, he glared at Eli, "Wal? What'chu got to say fer yo'self? After all, you'se on our claim!"

"Claim?" asked Eli, frowning as he looked around for any markers of a claim.

"That's what I said, claim." The man waved his hand to the side and toward the crest of the hill, "This hyar is our claim, an' the way I see it, you is trespassin'!" He turned to look at his partner who was leaning on the big boulder, nodding his head like he was snapping at flies on his chin. The partner was a mite taller than the talker, not nearly as wide, but he had not said a word and the way he was acting, Eli wondered if he could even talk. The partner had one piece of twine stretched across his shoulder that barely held up his raggedy britches and exposed his faded red union suit. He had a straw hat that looked like he had woven it out of some dried leaves of buffalo grass, and it drooped down to cover his ears and neck.

Eli shook his head in wonder as he looked from one man to the other, "First off, it's illegal to use a claim to block an established trail or roadway, and secondly, it doesn't make any difference if it is your claim or not, you're still obligated to sound a warning before you try to blow the whole mountain to kingdom come!" He took a deep breath, stepped back, and forced a bit of a grin, "Now, my name is Elijah McCain, and you are?" he asked as he looked from one to the other.

The talker nodded, "Uh, uh, I'm Rance 'n this," nodding to his partner, "is Gabby."

"Gabby?!" asked Eli, surprised at the nickname of a man that had yet to do anything but grunt. The partner nodded, grinning, and grunted as his tobacco mimicked Rance's and made its own trail through his scraggly beard.

Eli looked at the two men, "If there was a law against bein' stupid, you two would probably get life in prison!"

"Huh?!" asked Rance, looking at Gabby and back to Eli.

"You're lucky I didn't just shoot you, prob'ly should have, but I'm leaving now. If you know what's good for you, you'll sit right there on that rock until I'm out of sight. If I see you move, I'll pin you to that boulder with a hot piece of lead. NOW, SIT DOWN!" he shouted. The two men backstepped, hands raised, eyes wide, as they felt the rock behind them and sat back against it.

Eli swung back aboard the stallion, reined it around and called to the packhorse, "C'mon grey, we're leaving!" The dapple-grey mustang took to a trot to come close to the claybank stallion and Eli twisted around in the saddle to cast a snarling frown to the two prospectors. He shook his head, mumbling something about stupid people, and clasped legs to the stallion to kick him up to a trot and soon disappeared around the bend of the trail.

CHAPTER 2

FLATS

E li had been in the saddle since about midday the day before when he rode from Fort Benton. He was headed for Last Chance Gulch, about a week away, and where he hopefully might end his search. Since he left the Midwest just over two months ago, he had been on the trail of his two stepsons, twins Joshua and Jubal Paine, who had joined the Union Army, but deserted before the war ended. They ran off and headed west, according to the last letter home, and were determined to make their fortune in the goldfields of the west.

Eli was on a mission to fulfill a promise to his wife, the mother of the boys, a promise made on her deathbed, to 'bring my boys home.' Eli was a graduate of West Point and had a good record in the Union Army, first at Jefferson Barracks in St. Louis then Fort Laramie, and back east to be attached to the cavalry of General Sheridan. With considerable action in the war, he counted himself fortunate to only be wounded one time, and soon returned to the fight. After he was mustered out of the Union Army as a lieutenant colonel, he went to the bedside of his dying wife and agreed to fulfill her last wish. The first leg of his journey had taken him on a two-month stint on a steamboat stern-wheeler up the Missouri River from St. Louis to Fort Benton, Montana Territory. But it was aboard the *Louella* riverboat that he learned of the early days of the twins' journey, how they had worked on a steamboat that took them into Montana Territory where they joined up with a freighter and became muleskinners. But true to their practice of being fiddle-footed, they soon left the freighter and the last word Eli had was that they were bound for a claim in Last Chance Gulch where they were going to work for some established miners.

With a heavy sigh, he retreated from his reverie and looked round about, for this was new country to him. Although he had been stationed at Fort Laramie before the war, he had never been this far north, although the country was much the same. He made several inquiries before he left the Fort Benton area, giving special attention to a new friend and old mountain man that knew the country, Twofer. As was the custom of those that knew the West, he mentally mapped everything he was told and grinned as he watched the buffalo grass waving in the afternoon breeze and watched as a small herd of pronghorn antelope grazed contentedly about four hundred yards away. He knew the fastest animal on the plains would not be concerned about this one rider, for their eyesight was much better than a man, and their speed could put them far in the distance long before he could get near for a good shot. In the far distance, easily more than two to three miles, a wide blanket of brown slowly moved across the flat and he knew it to be a big herd of bison, probably numbering in the hundreds, perhaps more. This was the land of the bison, and they were a common sight. But he wasn't hungry and had no need of taking fresh meat, for he had a good pack of supplies aboard the dapple-grey gelding that followed free-rein behind him.

He was a man respected by most that met him, standing about a half-hand over six feet, weighing in at about 15 stone, or close to two hundred twenty pounds. Broad shouldered and always sitting tall in the saddle, his history of leading the cavalry was obvious as he rode the big claybank, or red dun, stallion that was a cross-breed of a Tennessee Walker and Morgan, that stood a good sixteen hands, broad chest, big rump, and soft eyes. The two, man and horse, had taken to one another the first time that Eli threw a saddle on the stallion, and they had been together ever since. Eli wore a linsey-woolsey grey shirt with a leather vest that hung loosely over his narrow hips that carried a holster with a Colt Army .44 caliber revolver and a sheathed Bowie knife that hung at the middle of his back, sometimes right next to the LeMat pistol tucked in his belt. A Winchester Yellowboy .44 caliber repeater lay in the scabbard beneath the right fender of his saddle and a Colt revolver shotgun, and .52 Caliber Spencer rifle were strapped on the pack of the little grey mustang.

This was the land of the Crow, a respected Native people that had kept their land from the onslaught of the neighboring Assiniboine and Blackfeet, and the people had been friendly with the white man. All the neighboring tribes, the Blackfeet, Assiniboine, Sioux, Gros Ventre, and Arikara had been a part of the 1851 Laramie Treaty, but the white men had been the first to break that treaty and now there were rumors of Indian wars and there had already been many skirmishes with different war parties and even renegades.

The discovery of gold in Montana Territory had just exacerbated the conflict between the encroaching white men and all the Natives and Eli knew that would only get worse with the many gold hunters, settlers, and others that were flooding into the traditional territory of the Native people. Although the politicians and generals were working on a new treaty, there was no reason to believe this one would be any more effective than the previous attempts at peace.

It was because of his knowledge and experience with many of the Native people that Eli always rode cautiously and tried to stay clear of the more heavily traveled roads, like the Mullan Road that was recently established from Fort Benton, south to the goldfields and west to eventually join the headwaters of the Columbia for the shipment of goods to the far western lands. Eli enjoyed the territory, always most content when he rode alone in new country, given time to enjoy the solitude with his Lord and all of His creation.

This land was the flatlands of the northern Great Plains. What many called flat, Eli knew the land to be rolling hills, terrain that was often misleading. Not really flat, but holding low-rising mesas, buttes, and bluffs, all covered with buffalo grass, Indian grass, sagebrush, gramma, rabbitbrush, and a variety of cacti. All enjoyed by the residents of the land, long-eared jackrabbits, coyotes, badgers, rattlesnakes, bull snakes, an occasional Gila monster, Swift Foxes that resembled midget coyotes, and an abundance of pronghorn antelope, buffalo or bison, and both white-tailed deer and mule deer. It was a land of plenty. Plenty of space, plenty of animals, and plenty of grass and cacti. But to Eli, it was a beautiful land of wide-open spaces and at least where he now rode, very few people.

Eli had kept to the lesser traveled trail that lay between the Mullan Road, also called the Benton Road and was also a toll road, that was built by the army for the transporting of supplies from Fort Benton to the Columbia River and on to Fort Walla Walla, Washington, and the Missouri River. He stayed in the flatlands above the river due to the many coulees, ravines, arroyos, and dry creek beds eroded by spring runoffs. But one coulee was too big to circumvent, and he was forced to keep to the trail that dropped into the bottom of the adobe hills and ravines. The green-bottomed trail twisted through the adobe and sandstone hills that were freckled with sage and scrub oak with scattered piñon. The bottom opened up and shoulders of the hills pushed back offering a wider valley bottom that pointed south to the wide alluvial plain that had pushed the Big Muddy around its broad bull head nose.

Rusty tossed his head and stopped, ears pricked and nostrils flaring as he looked to the mouth of the coulee. A herd of horses grazed at the edge of the river in a wide grassy meadow and the big stallion took in the smells of the herd. But Eli spotted two horsemen, Natives, and reached down to stroke Rusty's neck, "Easy boy, easy. We don't want to cause any trouble." But Eli knew he had already been spotted by the herd keepers when several of the horses turned and looked up the draw at the clay-bank stallion. A whinny came from a couple of the mares, and the guards, young men probably earning their warrior status, came together, motioning toward the man and talking. One of the young men wheeled his horse and took off to the north at a run.

Eli shook his head, "Well, boy, you've done it now!" and nudged the stallion forward. The grey packhorse stayed close, keeping the stallion between him and the herd. As he rounded the point of the butte, Eli first saw the smoke, then the many hide lodges of a camp of Natives. He knew he was in Crow country, and hoped this band was friendly. If not, he might be in a pretty difficult spot, but this was no time to weaken.

He saw several riders coming from the village, others following on foot, but none looking too friendly. He reined up and waited for the group to come close, and lifted his hand, palm open and facing them, and spoke, "*Bachiilápaatuua,* I come as a friend." This was what Twofer had taught him to say to the Crow. Although he knew very little of their language, he was more conversant in sign and used sign as he spoke.

One man stepped forward, returned his sign of peace, and spoke in his own tongue and sign, "Why are you here?"

"I am traveling south. I search for my two sons who left the war and came to this land."

"I am *Ba'suck'osh,* Goes Ahead. This is the village of the *Ashalaho* of the *Apsáalooke* people." He frowned at Eli, waiting for him to say his name as he stood stoically with arms across his chest.

Eli nodded, spoke and signed, "I am Elijah McCain, I come from the people to the east."

"We are here on a hunt for *bishée*, have you seen any buffalo?"

"Yes. I saw a big herd, far to the north." He turned and pointed to the flats above the river, and added, "Maybe one day's travel."

The leader let a grin split his face as he looked back to his people, nodding, and many of them talked excitedly to one another. Goes Ahead, who was also called *Walks Among the Stars,* turned back to Eli, "Our scouts will find them. They will return soon and tell us more. But what you have said is good news for my people. We have been hunting for this many days," he held up one hand, all fingers extended, "and my people are hungry for buffalo." He looked at Eli, stepped closer, and looked at the big stallion. He looked up at Eli, "You will stay with us this night. We will eat together." He grinned as he looked closer at Rusty, "Your horse will eat with our herd."

Eli chuckled, knowing exactly what the chief was thinking, but thought it alright for Rusty to have a little companionship for at least one night, as long as he did not wear himself out. Eli stepped down, walked beside the chief and did his best to talk and sign to be understood. It would be good to get to know this people, and they might even be some help in his search. He had learned long ago that the Natives know more about what might be happening and who was passing through their lands than most realized.

CHAPTER 3

ABSAROKA

A young man was motioned near and given the reins of Rusty, but Eli said, "I need to strip him first," and at the nod from Goes Ahead, the young man led the horses and man to a hide lodge with a matronly woman standing by the entry. She motioned to Eli to put his gear inside, stepped aside and went to the cookfire to tend to a pot that hung from a tripod of green willows. Eli grinned and quickly stripped both Rusty and the grey of their gear, stacking it all inside as the young man disappeared with the horses. When he emerged from the lodge, an attractive young woman motioned for him to follow.

The long shadows of the bluff stretched across the alluvial plain that held the Crow village as the sun dropped below the rise, beginning to paint the western sky in shades of brilliant orange, gold, and fringed with a pale pink. The cloudless sky had already begun to light the lanterns of the night, a few glimmering off his left shoulder, beyond the big bend of the Missouri River. Eli saw the diamonds of the night dancing on the rippling waters of the river as he walked behind the young maiden toward the central circle of the village.

The many Natives were busy, women tending cook-fires and readying for the night's feast, men bringing out the massive drum and a few smaller noisemakers, all preparing for the coming celebration. The young woman stopped beside the largest lodge of the village, a hide lodge tipi that was painted in scenes of battle and buffalo hunts with some symbols Eli did not understand but knew they would tell a story. As he admired the paint-ings, the entry flap was flipped aside and Goes Ahead came from the lodge, adorned in his split horn headdress and beaded tunic. His high moccasins held a similar pattern of beads as his tunic, and his fringed leggings had a long stripe of beads the length of the leg. He stood proudly before his lodge, head high, arms crossed, as he looked about his domain. He saw Eli, grunted, and motioned to a blanket with willow backrests, "We eat."

Eli stepped close to the backrests but remained standing until Goes Ahead seated himself. At the chief's motion, Eli sat down, crossed his legs, and leaned forward. All about the central compound, small cookfires glimmered, each attended by at least one woman who was tending to the cooking and others began serving those seated on blankets nearby. It was a joint but sepa-rate feast, and the excitement of a coming hunt was evident. In short order, most were finished with the feast and began adorning and arming themselves for the dance and as the drums began, led by the big drum where six men were busy beating out the cadence, the dancers began. The men, each armed with a long lance adorned with ribbons, strips of fur, and some with scalps, pantomimed a great buffalo hunt, dancing and chanting around in a great circle. The warriors wore only a breechcloth and leggings, but painted their chests, arms, and faces. Their hair was wound into a pompadour that was painted white, and the rest hung over their shoulders in long fur-wrapped hair pipes. Some had stuffed birds adorning their heads beside or before the pompadours. But when those that were covered with buffalo hides or wore the cape and skull cap with horns, joined the circle, the excitement rose to a feverish level as the hunters acted out the killing of great bulls and shouting their victorious chants.

Goes Ahead looked at his guest and asked in a mixture of Crow, English, and sign, "Have you hunted buffalo?"

"Yes. It is an exciting thing to hunt buffalo, and the meat is very good," replied Eli, watching the dancers.

"You will come with us?"

Eli knew he would be expected to join them for an invitation from the chief was a great honor, and to refuse could be seen as an insult, so he carefully chose his words as he responded. "What you say would be a great honor and I am humbled that you would ask, but if I fail to go find my sons, it would bring great grief and dishonor on my family and people. I must be on my way before the sun comes to find my sons and take them home to our family. If I delay, I may fail and that, too, would dishonor my family and my people."

The chief frowned, looked from Eli to the dancers and back again, "It is good to know you are a man of honor. It is good that you do this for your family. We will have other hunts and you will be welcome at our fire."

"I am grateful for your friendship, chief," replied a very relieved Eli. He breathed easier and turned his attention back to the dancers. He had not noticed when the young woman that had brought him to the chief's fire came behind him and seated herself. The dancers were tiring, and the drumbeats slowed, a signal for the women to join and the wives and intendeds of the dancers joined them as did other couples. They danced arm in arm, chanting together and showing an intimacy that Eli had never seen. He felt a tap on his shoulder and the young woman stood beside him, hands out, beckoning him to join her in the dance.

Eli looked from the girl to the chief, who nodded and grinned, and back to the girl. He rose to his feet and with her holding his hand and pulling him along, they joined the dance. He was surprised that he quickly caught the rhythm and was able to mimic the others as he danced, his arm around the waist of the girl, her arm around his. It was a stub toe, side shuffle kind of step, but it felt good to be with the people and to join in the dance. Many of the others watched him and the young woman, some scowling, others grinning, some laughing, but it was an enjoyable time and was over all too soon as the drum fell silent, and everyone went their own way. The girl looked at Eli, kept hold of his hand, and led him through the village and back to the lodge where he had left his gear.

Although she had spoken not a word before, she looked at Eli and spoke in perfect English, "I am told to make you welcome. What would you have of me?"

Eli grinned, "You speak well. Where did you learn English?"

"We had a missionary come to our village. His wife taught the girls, he taught the boys. They told us of many things, things I never knew, and it was a good time for us. He also taught of his God, the man Jesus, and what He did for all. He also told us of the gift of salvation and how we must believe, accept that Jesus paid for our sins, and offers us the free gift. Many of us did that. The missionary said we have a new life in Jesus, and we are to tell others."

Eli stepped back, shaking his head and smiling. "I am surprised and amazed to hear that. By the way, what is your name?"

"I am called Pretty Shield, after my mother who is also called Pretty Shield."

"I am Eli, Elijah McCain, and it is good to meet you Pretty Shield."

She dropped her eyes and timidly asked, "What can I do to make you comfortable?"

Eli grinned, "Well, you can start a warming fire in the lodge, spread the blankets for me, and then go to your lodge. I will leave early, probably before dawn, and be gone before the camp prepares for the buffalo hunt."

"I will do as you say, and I will return to fix you a meal before you go," stated Pretty Shield, ducking into the lodge before Eli could answer.

And Pretty Shield was true to her word and before Eli was up, she had a pan sizzling with timpsila, onions, and thin strips of venison. A pot of coffee danced on the rock at the edge of the fire. As the flames licked at the bottom of the pan, Eli recognized his pan and coffeepot, and smiled at the woman's ingenuity at using his gear. Eli stepped away from the tipi, stood tall and stretched and was surprised to see both horses tethered beside the lodge, watching him and his morning contortions.

Eli smiled at Pretty Shield, "I could get used to this! It's been a while since I woke to the smell of a cookfire with breakfast sizzling and coffee brewing and a pretty girl tending it all."

Pretty Shield smiled, "It will be ready soon."

"Thank you," answered Eli. He snatched up his jacket

and took to the trees for his quick morning trip and returned to the fire just as Pretty Shield poured his coffee. He accepted the coffee as she turned and began dishing up his food, motioning him to be seated on the blanket. After handing off his plate, she filled her own and sat nearby. Eli asked, "Did that missionary teach you about saying a prayer of thanks before you eat?"

She nodded, bowed her head, and listened as Eli prayed aloud, giving thanks for the day, the food, and the friendship of the people. When he said 'Amen,' Pretty Shield echoed him and looked up with a smile. "It is good to hear a man pray. My people do not do that, at least not aloud and with others."

Eli lifted his plate closer but asked, "Tell me about that, your people and what they believe."

"My people believe in one God, much like the whites, but he is called *Akbaatatdia*, One Who Has Made Everything. *Baaxpée* is what we call the power of God, but most just say *Xapáaliia* or medicine. When one says his medicine is good, or bad, or..." she shrugged.

"I've heard some refer to someone having good medicine, is that the same?" asked Eli, sipping on his coffee.

"Yes. When a young man wants to be a warrior, he must go on a vision quest to get his *Baaxpée*, his power, or medicine, which is loaned to him by *Akbaatatdia*. It is then they have their power, but they must have something to represent that medicine. That is why most will have a token or talisman, something that represents what they believe is the source of their power, something they saw or experienced on their vision quest."

"Do women also have a talisman or a vision?" asked Eli.

"Yes, but it is something that is never shared. To share it is to lose power," explained Pretty Shield. She looked thoughtful as she added, "One must always do their best, whatever it is they are asked to do, or choose to do. To do any less, is to offend the God of all power. It is called *Diakaashe*."

"That is a good way to live, always trying to do your best," mused Eli. "That is much the same, in a way, as the Christian faith. God wants us to always do our best and to treat others the way He would. It is then that we give honor to our God as well."

Pretty Shield smiled, stood and took his empty plate, poured him some more coffee and went about her work as Eli started gearing up the horses. Each one contemplated the thoughts of the other and learned from one another.

As Eli swung aboard Rusty, the sun was just beginning to paint the eastern sky in muted shades of pink that faded to a pale yellow and into the dusty blue of the early morning sky. He looked at Pretty Shield, smiled, "It has been good to know you Pretty Shield. I hope we will see one another again."

"I too, ask for this, Eli, Elijah McCain," she replied, looking up at the big man on the big horse and smiled. She watched as he rode from the village and turned up the coulee to the trail that would take him south and hopefully to the goldfields of Last Chance Gulch.

CHAPTER 4

COMPANY

The trail lifted out of the big coulee by way of a twisting route between the rugged piñon freckled buttes. The flats atop the plains showed the wrinkled coulee that stretched west for about a mile and bent south and stretched out of sight beyond the rolling hills of the buffalo grass covered plains. The morning was cool, the breeze light, and a herd of antelope watched the stranger on the big horse from afar. The Mullan Road was beyond the coulee and the flatlands appeared undisturbed by man. It was an easy trail he followed, and when the sun shone bright off his left shoulder, he came to another deep coulee that forced the trail to the west. He had only come about five miles when he saw a slow-moving dust cloud before him that he guessed was from a southbound stage on the road.

And he was right. He spotted the red painted Concord stage with its bright yellow wheels behind a six-up hitch of horses as it dipped down into the now shallow draw and was belched out the far side. But that was not the only moving dust cloud, coming along slower were two wagons, both drawn by a four-up hitch of mules with riders beside them. As he neared, all he saw were men, prospectors probably, all of whom watched him as he neared. Eli counted four riders, four more men on the wagons, and no sign of women or children. Eli lifted a hand in a bit of a wave and greeted the travelers, "Howdy, fellas!"

A barrel-chested man aboard a big plow horse looking animal reined around to face him, the wagons not slowing, and growled, "What'chu want?!"

"Want? Nothin', just bein' friendly," answered Eli, dropping both hands to the saddle horn as he reined up Rusty, the packhorse stopping beside them.

"We ain't the friendly sort. Keep yore distance!" he demanded, jerking the head of the horse around and digging his heels into the animal's ribs. Without so much as a glance back, the big man caught up to his companions and grumbled something to the others, prompting them to glance back to Eli, turn away, and keep on the road.

Eli shook his head, *Friendly bunch, but a bunch to watch out for, my guess is they're up to no good. Prob'ly headed for the goldfields and lookin' for trouble. They look to be the sort that if they can't make it the easy way, they'll force themselves on others and take what they want. Yup, trouble.* He nudged Rusty forward choosing to take to the road just long enough to make the crossing of the coulee, then he would return to the trail he originally followed.

The trail bent back to the southwest and away from the road. He had seen several cairns alongside the trail, some appearing to be so old he guessed them to be from the previous century. Rocks stacked, marked, weathered and more, that held secrets of long-ago travelers from faraway lands and nearby villages. The trail was worn, even across wide swaths of sandstone, and few tracks of recent travelers had weathered the winds of the plains. He felt alone, the solitude comforting, and he talked with his Lord as they traveled, accompanied only by the whisper of the morning breeze, the rustle of tall grasses, the clatter of hooves, and the creak of the saddle leather.

But his reverie was short lived when a long-eared jackrabbit scampered from under a big sage, chased by a hungry coyote and Rusty spooked enough to make a sudden stop with stiff legs, dropped head, and pricked ears and with a snort the big stallion jerked backward, making Eli bury the saddle horn in his gut and his face part the red mane on the stallion's neck. But it was just a one jump spook, and the stallion snorted his contempt at the tail of the coyote as it disappeared under another sage. Eli sat erect, shaking his head, "You're gonna be the death of me yet, you lop-eared cayuse!" he growled, but reached down to stroke the stallion's neck and calm him down.

They had come about three miles since the last coulee crossing when the earth opened up again in a wide and deep gash that scarred the land, but the trail continued and took to a shallow gulley that held the meandering trail as it dropped into the bottom. The big stallion quickened his pace when he saw green in the bottom and apparently smelled water. As the ravine opened into the wider coulee bottom, they rounded a point and five white-tail deer, one big buck among them, scattered as they waved their white flags behind them. The horses lifted their heads, pricked their ears, but were not alarmed and did not miss a step as they made their way to the spring-fed stream in the bottom.

The big stallion dropped his nose into the clear, cold

water of the little stream as Eli swung down between the dun and the grey and scooped up a handful of fresh water. The breeze whispered down the draw toward the river and Eli got a whiff of foul-smelling stench. He came to his feet just as the grey spooked and jumped across the little stream, exposing Eli to the skunk and caught the stench straight on as the striped cousin to the family cat twisted his back and let loose with his only defense. Eli staggered back, falling into the water and splashing about, trying to escape, just as Rusty leaped over him and the stream to get away. The thrashing and splashing sent the skunk scampering into the brush and Eli sat chest deep in the water hole, shaking his head and gasping for breath. He twisted around to see both horses standing a little spread-legged, heads down and he was certain they were laughing at him.

He slapped the water, dug up handfuls of mud and covered his face, neck, shirt, and everything else he could reach. He stood, turned to look at the horses who seemed to shake their heads at him as they bobbed their heads and backed away. He snatched up his hat that had sailed off his head when he fell, stomped to the horses, and grabbed up the reins and the lead rope that was looped around the neck of the grey, and started upstream to escape from the lingering stench. After about fifty yards, he spotted a wide grassy spot, tethered and stripped the horses, and grabbed his bedroll that held his change of clothes, and returned to the water. He stood askance on the bank, looking about, and dropped the bedroll. He meandered about, snatching whatever he thought might help with his new-found perfume. Anything and everything that had a bloom, he gathered. Walking away from the stream, he found sage, rabbit-brush, and some prickly pear cactus. Carefully picking several palms of the cacti to add to his collection, he went to some yucca, dug around it and gathered the roots for soap. He returned to the stream and dropped his bounty.

Stripping off his clothes and leaving them in a pile at water's edge, he waded into the cold water and began his ministrations. Digging at the mud with his toes and hands, he soon gave the appearance of a mud dog, head to toe he was covered with a layer of rich black mud. He rubbed it into his skin as much as he could stand, feeling like he was stripping off a layer of skin, but it had to be done. He stretched out in the stream, rinsed off the mud and began making poultices of mashed flowers and leaves that he used as a sponge to rub into his skin and hair. Once that was finished, he carefully peeled off the layer of skin and needles of the prickly pear and smeared the gelatinous middle over his body. It would serve as both a cleansing and healing salve.

He sat down on the grassy bank and began stripping the roots of the yucca and smashed the roots into a sudsy pulp and walked back into the water. The yucca root was a commonly used soap by the Natives, and he scrubbed his body clean, once, twice, and three times. With a final rinse, he came from the water, and with a long stick, shoved his dirty clothes into the stream, weighting them down with a rock. He would dry off with a blanket and get dressed before going for more yucca root to wash his clothes.

He sat down on a big rock, shaking his head and laughing at himself. He looked at the horses who stood staring at him, ears pricked, and unmoving. "What're you looking at?" he asked, laughing, "You were no help at all!"

He stood, breathed deep, and thought he had

succeeded in ridding himself of the stench, but only time and fresh air would tell. For now, he needed to make a better camp, round up something to eat, and fetch some more yucca for his other clothes, that is, *if* he chose to keep them. It might just be easier to leave them where they lay.

He soon had a little fire going, being careful to fan all the smoke his way, and put the last of his pork belly in the pan with the timpsila. The coffeepot was dancing on the rocks and the smell of fresh coffee was refreshing after the afternoon's experience. After the food was ready, he sat the pan aside, put some alder branches on the fire, and again fanned the smoke his way. Taking deep breaths, he still had the smell of skunk in his nose, but he fought against it and hoped to be rid of it soon. *Reckon I'll have to stay away from people for a few days.* He glanced at the horses who were lazily grazing, *And I hope you two will be a little more tolerant. I ain't looking to do any walking!*

CHAPTER 5

THE RAPIDS

He made a bed of piñon and cedar boughs, both known for their strong if not pungent fragrance, but he knew he needed all the help he could get because he couldn't hardly stand himself, even while he slept. He had scrubbed his clothes with mud, yucca root, and beat them on the rocks and did it all over again. The linsey-woolsey shirt and wool gabardine trousers and the holey red union suit all were spread on the branches of the piñon trees that surrounded his little camp and had absorbed their share of the alder smoke. *If that doesn't get rid of the smell, it'll prob'ly make me smell like old jerky, but that's not near as bad as fresh skunk!* He laughed at himself and knew it would be something he would not soon forget.

He stretched out on the pine boughs, his thin blanket offering some semblance of a bed, and with hands clasped behind his head, he looked at the stars and spent some time talking to his Lord. He started to roll to his side, when he remembered a conversation he had with Captain Marsh, the captain of the riverboat

Louella, the boat that he had traveled on from St. Louis. "Those two boys that I remember, left our boat at Dauphin Rapids and took up with a freighter by the name of Paquette. Those freighters are like vultures, always waiting beside the rapids or falls for a boat that has too much draft and will offload their goods for the freighters to haul on to Fort Benton. There's others that wait for the boats that travel upriver from Benton but can't make it past the falls. Those are the real vultures, they know the captains have no choice but to offload their cargo, or take it back to Benton, and they charge double. But if I was you, I'd be lookin' at Colter Falls, that'd be the easternmost one and there's never been a steamer of any kind that I know of get past that one. There's a road for the freighters on the north side."

Eli grinned, nodded, and rolled to his side to get some sleep. He would make an early start in the morning to get to the lower falls and maybe find some freighters that would know about his boys.

———

TALL GRASSES TICKLED the belly of the big stallion; wheatgrass, buffalo, Indian, bluestem, and many other varieties were abundant on the great plains of Montana Territory, and it was easy to see the recent passage of riders. But the land before him, illumined by the early morning sun, danced to the melody of the whispering wind, choreographed by the Creator, and showing waves like the great oceans. There were places when Eli, mounted on his claybank stallion, could reach the tops of the grasses as he pushed through the waving mass, which Rusty occasionally snatched a mouthful as he passed. The grey packhorse was lazily following behind, letting the big horse part the way before them.

The sun was barely above the eastern horizon when Eli was brought up short by the narrow road that parted the waves of grass. He looked at the road that showed fresh tracks of several mules and wagons, all sign showing they had passed the night before and had not returned on the same road. Eli stood in his stirrups and looked in the direction of the wagons' travel, saw the scar of the Big Muddy and with a slow nod of realization, he knew these were freighters headed to the lower rapids, probably the Colter Falls, and were looking for a load of freight, either consigned or solicited. Assuming the freighters had come from the Mullan Road to the west, probably from the goldfields still to the south, he reined the claybank onto the narrow road, just two tracks really, and started toward the river. As he considered what he might encounter, he frowned and began searching for a promontory that he might use to have a better look-see before revealing himself.

In the Great Plains, the Missouri River had cut its way across the plains and the wide scar, showing about a half-mile wide on both banks, was carved deep and rugged by the many runoffs that carried the mud and silt of each spring into the big river to be carried on its way to the east and south. Those rugged banks that rose over two hundred feet before reaching the flatlands of the plains, were marked by ravines, coulees, gullies, and arroyos, all names of runoff carvings.

The narrow roadway followed by the wagons before him, dropped off the edge of the bluff and rode a ridge between arroyos, before taking the lesser of hillsides with an easy side slope, then bumped over a bench and dropped into the alluvial flats that held Sulphur Spring, easily identifiable by the strong odor. Eli left the road before it crossed the bench, took an old game trail that split a pair of smaller buttes, and led to the crest of a higher hilltop that would suit his purposes for a promontory. He stopped in the bottom of the arroyo, picketed the horses in a thicket of piñon, and choosing his Spencer over the Winchester, and with the cased binoculars hanging over one shoulder, he started up to the crest of the grass and scrub oak covered butte.

Eli bellied down atop the butte, choosing a slab of rock that lay between the scrub oak brush and slipped the binoculars from the case. He had already spotted three wagons, backed up to the gravelly bank of the river, but the mules and horses had been picketed on some grass in the bottom of the draw that sided the narrower draw below a small pool of water that lay below a spring. A slight breeze carried the smell of sulphur and Eli knew it was the spring Twofer had mentioned. "It's a li'l spring that stinks sumpin' fierce, but they believe it's got healin' powers. Now, I don' know 'bout that, but it's been said that ol' Meriwether Lewis got some of its water to heal a sick Sacajawea, the Shoshoni woman that was his guide," the old mountain man cackled at the telling, "But if'n you get close, you'll know it, that's fer shore'n certain. Ain't nuthin' smells that bad 'cepin' them big geysers in Colter's Hell!"

Eli grinned at the remembrance and lifted the binoculars to search the land below. Three wagons, two the same, one with higher sideboards and a sign hanging on the side. But the sign was illegible, especially from this distance. He frowned as he scanned the camp where the freighters had apparently spent the night. He looked at the horses that were picketed near the mules, frowned as he thought he recognized the bigger of the bunch as the big plow-horse-looking animal that was ridden by the unfriendly man with the two wagons that he had spotted the day before. He lowered the glasses, looking at the camp, where the men were gathered by a cookfire, and with a deep furrowed brow, he slowly scanned the gathering, looking as best he could at each man. The day before, he only had a good look at the big man, the gruff, heavily whiskered, plug-ugly type of man. But the big brute was easily recognized when he stood and stomped away from the fire, hurling orders and insults over his shoulder to the others.

Eli counted the men, remembering the day before, there were eight men, none but the big man familiar. Four on horseback, four on the wagons. But with another wagon, there should be more, but he counted only eight men. Eli frowned, wondering, *Now where'd they get that other wagon and mules?*

As he watched, he heard the long blast of a steam whistle and shifted his binoculars to look downstream. A side-wheeler packet was chugging up the river. Smaller than the *Louella* that he came up on, the boat was a freight packet that had little space for passengers and was mostly used for freight, although they allowed deck passengers for the right price. The boat nosed into the bank, scraping on the gravelly shore, the roustabout jumping off and taking the mooring rope to tie it off. The gangplank dropped and a man with a kepi-style cap started down the plank, waving at the men on shore who were walking toward the boat. Within a short while, the conversation ended and the crew of the boat and the men of the wagons began unloading the cargo from the boat and hoisting it up onto the wagons.

The sun was high overhead when the cargo transfer was complete, although not all the freight could be taken by the three wagons and some large boxes were stacked near some buckbrush and covered. The big man stood shaking hands with the pilot from the boat, gestured to the stack of unloaded gear and nodded, probably agreeing to watch over the cargo and come back with another wagon. He accepted the papers, signed off on some, and each turned away to his own task. Eli watched as the boat backed away, turned downstream, and disappeared. The men of the wagons waved, then looking at one another started laughing and slapping each other on the back as they went for the mules and horses.

Eli had a familiar prickly sensation that seemed to crawl up his back as he continued watching, *Something's not right here.* He turned away, searched the area all around, making certain there was no other threat, then looked back at the men below. They had harnessed and hooked up the mules to the three wagons, and with two men on horses, the others on the wagons and the extra animals trailing behind, they started up the zigzag road to the crest of the wide plateau above the river.

Eli slipped and slid down the steep slope to the horses, led them down the draw to the little stream for a good drink and to bide his time to give the wagons time to get further away, then mounted up and started up the road. He would follow this bunch until he could find out just what their gig was, he knew it was not right, but he wasn't too sure just exactly what was happening. He had a good idea, but…he shrugged, nudging Rusty to take the road at a good pace.

It was about five or six miles to the junction of this little road and the Mullan Road. Eli easily followed the trail of the wagons and guessed they would turn on the Mullan to the south, bound for the goldfields. The grassy flats offered little cover and he kept his distance but frowned when he saw the circling of turkey buzzards. Initially, he thought little of it, for any dead creature or remains of one, would attract the vultures, but that feeling came again. He reined up, watching the circling black birds and nudged Rusty that direction. He soon came on what had attracted the buzzards and several other carrion eaters. The bodies of four men and the burned remains of a freight wagon were the center of attention for coyotes, ravens, magpies, whisky jacks, a badger, and a skittish fox.

They had apparently made camp off the road, two big piñon offered a little cover, and the men had been attacked in their sleep. The burned wagon was missing a wheel that lay off to the side, two broken spokes showing. Anyone would assume it was the work of renegade Indians, but Eli knew better. The sign of one wagon and a team of mules that trampled the grasses to get to the narrow road to the river was obvious. There was sign of other mules that were driven off through the grasses, but nothing else.

He reined away from the carnage, shaking his head, thinking, *Pretty sneaky. Who would suspect thieves to have wagons? They make a deal, sign the papers, and haul away all the goods.* He shook his head as he returned to the road, determined to find out just what these road agents would do and if there would be any stopping them.

CHAPTER 6

TRAIL

Dusk was beginning to drop its curtain when the wagon tracks left the road. Eli stopped and leaned over Rusty's shoulder to look closer, lifted his eyes in the direction of the tracks and saw the line of green that marked the riverbank of the Big Muddy. The glow of a campfire showed among the trees and Eli looked about for some cover. He wanted a closer look, either now or with first light, he wanted to know each of these men well enough to spot them anywhere. He had a hunch he was about to launch himself on a long trek to deal justice to this band of outlaws. He was reminded of the words of his father, "The only thing it takes for evil to prevail is for good men to do nothing. Son, you can't always leave justice to those that are carrying a badge or a baton or wearing judge's robes."

He pointed Rusty through the deep grass to a low knoll that lifted out of the flatlands, showing its bald head in the dim light and obscuring the river. Tethering the horses in a cluster of piñon, he started through the grass to the crest of the little knoll, as he neared the top he bellied down and worked his way to the top.

He was surprised to see a farmhouse, a big barn, corrals, and a couple of outbuildings. He lifted his binoculars and began his scan. The two corrals were full of mules, the barn door was closed and the campfire he saw from the road glimmered through the trees nearer the river. Lights showed in the farmhouse, but no horses were at the hitchrail, he could only assume that one or more of the men called this home.

There was movement at the campfire, but the trees were too dense to get a look at any of the men near the fire. He moved his field glasses back to the farmhouse and saw shadows in the windows, but the curtains masked the interior. One man, a big man, was in a rocking chair on the covered porch, but the light was dim, and the roofline obscured the man. As he watched, the door opened, lancing the coming darkness with a shaft of light, and the man in the rocker went inside, closing the door behind him. Eli frowned as he lowered the binoculars, tried to pierce the dim light with his naked eyes, but saw nothing but darkening shadows. With a deep sigh, he crabbed back from the crest and returned to his horses.

Choosing to have a cold camp and keep his presence unseen, he stripped the horses and rolled out his blankets. With a handful of jerky, he crawled into his bedroll and stretched out. His head lay in the seat of the saddle as he looked at the sky, stars slowly lighting their lanterns, and the sliver of moon creeping over the eastern horizon, and shook his head, remembering many nights just like this but with the roar of cannon in the distance and the smell of gunpowder and death in the air. Just the whisper of a breeze, the cry of the nighthawk, and some big old owl asking his usual question of the darkness, brought a sense of peace and quiet to his spirit. He whispered his prayer to his Savior and soon dropped off to sleep.

————

ELI ROSE before the sun showed its face in the east, but the thin line of grey began to blush pink as he crawled through the grass for another look at the farm. Nothing was stirring, but a light came on in one window as a man pushed through the door, a pail and a basket in hand. Eli tried to get a better look at the man, but all he could tell was he was not the big man on the porch the night before. A floppy felt hat shadowed his face as he walked briskly to the barn, probably to milk the cow and maybe gather any eggs from the chickens.

Eli moved the glasses to scan the woods where the campfire had shown the presence of the others, but nothing. No activity, no smoke, no animals moving about, nothing. Eli frowned, turned back to the barn, and watched. Two men came from behind the barn and entered the corral to drive the mules into a fenced grassy meadow behind the barn. As he looked, he could see the meadow was bounded by the thick woods on the river side, and an embankment at the flank of the butte, a natural enclosure that would hold the mules and the few horses.

As he scanned the buildings, corrals, and the rest of the property, he could tell the farm was new, maybe a couple years old at most, but the field in front of the house had been plowed and planted. It appeared to be two fields, different crops, but the little flags of corn were showing in the one, just sprouts in the other. It appeared to have the makings of a good farm, the hard work was evident, and the farmer was probably proud. But it did not explain the activity of the freighters, or the outlaws, whichever they were. Eli shook his head and crabbed back from the crest and returned to the horses. He had decided he would leave before anyone could spot him. He would have to figure this out some other time. For right now, he was headed to Last Chance Gulch.

———

FOUR OF THE men gathered around the campfire in the cottonwoods near the Big Muddy, had been together since before the war. They had been prisoners in "The Walls" the notorious prison in Baton Rouge, Louisiana and were part of the convict leasing program before the war started, but the need for soldiers in the Confederacy occasioned their release to join the army. There had been ten men in the first group, but after surviving some of the early battles, five were killed at Gettysburg, prompting the desertion of the remainder. Led by the big man, Ludvik Kowalski, they had taken up the way of guerrillas and bulled their way west by forcing themselves on others. Although Ludvik had been called many things behind his back, none survived to call him anything but boss or Vik, short for his name. All those that followed him had long ago learned to do as they were told, he was too big and too mean to buck, and they had seen the results of his lost temper too many times as bodies lay scattered around him.

"I don't get it! There's barrels of whiskey in those wagons, ain't one more or less gonna make any difference!" grumbled Gunther Koch, most often called Gunner, one of the original gang. "He ain't been this persnickety a'fore!" sniveled the towheaded man. He leaned down to pick up a stick to throw in the fire, the gold glow of the flames showing the broad shoulders heavy with muscle under a tight stretched linen shirt. He was as tall as Ludvik, but not as heavy nor as experienced at rough-and-tumble fighting, nor near as mean nor willing to kill.

"He wants us all to stay stone-cold sober. I dunno what he's got planned, but I'm thinkin' it's bigger'n anything we done before," answered Karl Fischer, the number two man in the bunch. He and Ludvik had been together since before "The Walls" and Karl had always been faithful to the big man. "Look, you know he's a lot smarter than he looks or acts, and he ain't never done us wrong before, so, I'm tellin' you to just stick it out and we'll all be better off'n we been before."

"Well, what 'bout them women? There's two o' them an' both're good-lookin' women, an' we ain't been 'round no women since…I dunno when, it's been so long!" whined Grant Lewis, the one who fancied himself as a pretty boy ladies' man. "He gonna keep 'em to himself?"

Karl shook his head, "Women are gonna be the death of you, boy!"

"Mebbe, but at least I'll die happy!" snickered Grant.

"I know you and Clark there are the last to join up with us, but you know the boss don't want any whiskey or wimmen to interfere with us doin' a job. An' he says this'n is gonna net us more money than anything else, so, I'm not just speakin' for the boss, I'm speakin' for myself. If you or anyone else does anything to mess this up, the boss won't *have* to take care of you, I'll do it my ownself!" growled Karl, snarling as he looked around the circle at each man.

A quiet man sat at the edge of the glow of the fire, sharpening a big Bowie knife that was his favorite weapon. He was an expert at knife fighting, throwing, and silent killing, seeming to enjoy the killing most. His eyes flashed at Karl, "Or you could let me do it!" he snarled and followed it with a chilling cackle as he laughed without missing a stroke of his knife on the whetstone. Antonio Rodriguez, known simply as the Mex, carried more knives than any knew—in both boots, behind his back in his belt, hanging between his shoulder blades, and tucked behind his belt between the two silver-handled Colt pistols that sat in black holsters with silver conchos. No one had seen him use the pistols, but most had seen the results of his knives.

Karl looked around the group, "We better turn in, we'll start early tomorrow to get to the goldfields."

"We takin' the wagons?" asked Grant.

"No, the boss'll let us know who's goin' where. We need to find the best place to get rid o' the wagons for the most money and that means we gotta find some store or sumpin' that'll buy it. Like he says, what with all the gold miners brimmin' wit' money, and the stores willin' to charge what they can, we shouldn't have any trouble."

There was some grumbling, but most were willing to ride things out in hopes of a good payday. But they also knew that all the 'big jobs' had netted them very little, but at least they were well away from where they were known and wanted. With a few glances to one another, the men moved away from the fire and went to their blankets, hopeful for a better tomorrow.

In the barn, Jonesy and Walters were in the hay loft, their blankets rolled out on the soft hay as they turned in after letting the horses and mules out onto the grassy meadow behind the barn. "So, Jonesy, you know the boss better'n me, you think this'll amount to anythin'?" asked Lloyd Walters, another of the men that joined up after they left the Confederacy.

"I dunno, Lloyd. The boss an' Karl like to think they're big-time outlaws, an' I know we been together for a while. All I can say is, we ain't missed too many meals like what we was doin' in the war, an' that's better. But there ain't no coin jinglin' in my pockets and I ain't got no idee what might be happenin' tomorrow, much less any time in the future. I used to think I'd like to have me a farm, kinda like this'n, but I don't reckon that'll ever be."

"I dunno 'bout'chu, but I ain't no namby-pamby sissy britches, an' I done my share o' killin' in the war, but what that man did to them freighters, an' settin' 'em on fire, that just…" he shrugged as a chill went up his spine at the memory.

"Don't let him hear you questionin' anythin' like that. He'd just as soon kill you as look at'chu, just like he did them," warned Jonesy. He and Lloyd Walters had kind of buddied up and occasionally confided with one another.

"I'm a little concerned 'bout them women in the house too. He don't like anybody else gettin' 'round women, but what about him?" asked Lloyd.

"I ain't known him to go back on what he demands of the men, but I heard tell that was why he was in prison. Seems some women in a house, you know what I mean, they made fun o' him bein' so big, so he beat the women and tore the house down around 'em. He didn't kill 'em, but that's the only thing that kept 'em from hangin' him. He got a firsthand taste of the way most men think about women, even those that do business in places like that. It ain't a good thing to mistreat a woman! He learned that, and mebbe that's why he tries to keep the men away from 'em."

"What's one man doin' with two women anyway?" asked Lloyd, thinking of the two women in the farmhouse. There was only one man, the farmer, and no kids, but two women.

"I think I heard 'em say the dark-haired one was his wife, and the other'n with the lighter hair, was her sister."

"I still don't like it. I seen the way the boss looks at 'em, an…"

"Ummhmm, but we best stay out of it."

"Huh, I'd hafta agree with that. Let's get some shut-eye," mumbled the sleepy Lloyd, turning away from his partner and wiggling a way into the hay to get comfortable.

CHAPTER 7

GOLDFIELDS

P rospect holes dotted the countryside. Most of the would-be prospectors knew little or nothing about gold and where it could be found, so random holes were dug into hillsides, creekbanks, anywhere someone thought it worthwhile to try their luck. Most of the holes were no more than a few feet deep, and just big enough for a man to get into, before it was abandoned, leaving the hole and the dug out dirt and rock to scar the hillsides. Along every creek, and even in the dry creek beds, gold seekers were searching for any paydirt. Wherever there was water, a rocker box had a prospector attached to the handle, making time like an organ grinder. As the water spilled out and the riffles held promise, the man would bend over and finger through the mud like a long-ago youngster making mud pies.

Eli shook his head as he rode past the gold-blinded prospectors, many looking up suspiciously at the passing stranger, but quickly turned back to their work as he moved away, leaving tiny dust devils at his passing. He had been on the road for the past three days, camping out near the river in the thick cottonwoods by night, but still eager to work toward the heart of the goldfields, the growing village now called Helena. The sun was bright and the warmth on his back was pleasant and the long-legged claybank stallion stretched out at a quick pace, his hooves clattering on the hard packed roadway, but lifting dust as he passed. The dapple-grey packhorse kept pace with the big stallion, running free rein off his right hip.

The rattle of trace chains and the clatter of many more hooves came from behind him and Eli nudged Rusty to the shoulder of the road, looking back to see the rapid approach of a stagecoach with a six-up team of horses making time towards Helena. Eli reined up to let the coach pass, nodded to the driver and messenger, and heard a shout from within as a man stuck his hand out to wave. Eli frowned, shook his head, and wondered at who would be hollering at him, although he was certain he heard his name called as the coach passed.

The hills rose on both sides of the road that followed Little Prickly Pear Creek through the piñon dotted country. Eli waited just a few moments for the dust to settle from the passing of the Concord stagecoach, then nudged Rusty on as he lifted his eyes to the sun. He guessed there would be a stage station soon, knowing they were spaced out about every fifteen or so miles, allowing for fresh teams to continue their journey. But it was nearing midday and he thought the stage would be stopping for a meal.

It was just a short while later that the road made a dog-leg bend around a knee of a hill as it followed the little creek, and the narrow valley opened to show a low-topped log building with a barn and big corrals behind. A faded board sign read, *Lyons Creek Stage Stop*. The red and yellow Concord stage sat idle while hostlers were busy changing the teams, but all the passengers were gathered at a long table under a wide-spread canopy that stretched out beside the stage station. As Eli reined up in front of the station, a matronly woman spoke, "If yore stoppin' to eat, better git'chu a seat 'fore it's all gone! Cost a dollar an' you pay 'fore you sit!"

Eli nodded, looking at the woman as he started to swing down from the stallion. When his feet touched ground, he dug a dollar coin from his britches pocket and flipped it to the woman who deftly caught it and stuffed it into her apron without spilling a drop of the coffee in the big pot she carried. He led the horses to the water trough, let them have a good drink, but pulled them away and picketed them on a patch of grass by the creek. He loosened the cinches, gave them a rub on the neck, and turned back to the dinner table.

As he neared, he saw an uplifted hand that motioned him near, and he saw a familiar face. The man sat next to a woman, both of whom were smiling and nodding as he came close and offered him a seat beside the man. The man extended his hand, "Good to see you, Eli."

Eli shook his hand but the frown on his face told the man he did not recognize him, but a smile from the man told him it must have been on the riverboat. Eli sat down and grinned at the man, "It must have been on the *Louella*, right?"

"Oui, oui. I am Martine Beaumont, and this is my wife, Amélie. We were on the boat, and we are going to set up a mercantile store in Helena."

Eli nodded, smiling, as he filled his plate from the passing dishes, "I remember now. It was Constance Wellington that introduced us." He paused as he took a sip of the hot coffee, then continued, "So, are things progressing for your store?"

"Oui, oui. We are hoping to get our shipment of goods soon. In the meantime, we will get the building ready for the store. It is a good building, built from stone, and has a bank in the other side. I spoke to Samuel Hauser who opened the bank and leased half of the building from him."

"And this shipment of goods, how is it coming?" asked Eli, trying to be both curious and casual as he inquired.

"Oh, one shipment is already there, but the second shipment is larger, and is coming by packet up the river. It will be met by a freighter and carried overland to Helena. It should be here soon," explained Martine.

Eli nodded, focusing on the food which was nothing more than a stew of sorts, but the bread was good, and the pot was big, and the coffee was black and hot. Most stage stations were not known for good food but were known for high prices on the fare. But it saved him having to deplete his own supplies and take the time to cook a meal in the middle of the day, which was not a common practice for him. Eli pushed his plate back, looked at Martine, "If the mercantile doesn't work out for you, you might consider putting in a café. With these prices," nodding around the table, "you could get rich in no time!"

Martine chuckled, smiled at his wife, "We have considered that. My wife is an excellent cook, and we might do that as well."

"Are there other mercantiles in Helena?" asked Eli.

"There is at least one, but by now, there could be more. It is a booming area, so many gold seekers, other businesses, and such, but it is also a lawless area. That is bad."

"Have you been there before?" asked Eli, curious as to how he would know so much about the town.

"No, but I have talked to many travelers, in St. Louis, on the boat, at Fort Benton, and even here on the stage. There are some on the stage that have been there and other places." He nodded to two men at the end of the table, "They say they have a successful mine and had to go east to order the big equipment to do more. Now they return to ready their mine for much more. They were there at the beginning. They have two partners that stayed there and continued working while they went to St. Louis. They," nodding to the two men, "are D.J. Miller and John Crabb."

"Well, you said it was a lawless land, and indeed it is. I understand there have also been some hold-ups of the packet riverboats. You remember the problems we had with the gunrunners and more, but there are those that rob the boats and the freighters also."

"Oui, I know. We are fortunate that we already have a shipment waiting for us in Helena, and if the second shipment makes it, all the better. Everything we have is in this venture and we simply must make it work. But I did take out insurance with INA. I used to work for them in Philadelphia and not many know they do that, but, well, we have so much in this, it was worth the extra. But, if it does not make it, I have no idea what we might do, but…" he shrugged, trying to make the best of things.

Eli nodded, "My family was in shipbuilding and shipping, so I understand about insurance. We did business with Lloyd's of London whenever we had a special cargo.

That was very smart of you to do the insurance, I don't think many do that, at least not out west."

Martine nodded, frowned, and asked, "But didn't I hear that you were searching for your sons? Have you found them?"

Eli turned stoic, shaking his head, "Not yet. Although I am hopeful. The captain of the *Louella* told about them taking work with a freighter named Paquette, and I talked with a couple men with that company. They said the boys left for the goldfield to work with a miner there. So, maybe I'll find them among the many men that are digging for gold."

"Tell me about the boys, perhaps we will see them come into our store," suggested Martine, his wife nodding her agreement.

Eli pulled the leather case that held the tintype, flipped it open to show Martine and Amélie and began to describe the boys, twins, who resembled their mother and their natural father. "Their father was killed before the boys were born and I was asked to look after his wife and children and was privileged to marry her before the boys were born. I'm the only father they've known, but they took their father's name, Joshua and Jubal Paine."

Amélie held the tintype, smiling and looked up at Eli, "They are fine-looking boys. I'm sure you're proud of them."

"Yes, but regrettably I was not home much, the military had me out west and then the war came and…" he shrugged, "but the boys weren't cut out for the army and before the war was over, they took off for the West. And now, I search."

"We will always watch for them. Twin boys should be easily found, but we," nodding to his wife, "will be in prayer for you and the boys," offered Martine.

"That would be appreciated," answered Eli, standing and stepping back from the table just as the messenger from the stage called for everyone to get aboard.

Eli shook Martine's hand, tipped his hat to Amélie, and watched as the passengers climbed aboard. With the burgeoning town of Helena and the prosperous gold diggings, the stage was loaded. Nine passengers, the Beaumonts included, were inside, four more sat up top. Eli watched as the jehu cracked his long whip over the heads of the horses and the animals leaned into their collars. The stage rocked back on the thoroughbraces and with a tuft of dust, the stage was on the road bound for Helena, the next stop for the weary travelers.

Eli went to his horses, tightened the cinch on his saddle and the pack saddle, swung aboard and started on the road. They would make Helena about dark, but he had not decided whether to pitch camp somewhere or to get a room at the hotel, providing there was one. He chuckled to himself and with a deep breath, enjoyed the fresh air and the scarcity of people, even though there were signs of prospecting just about everywhere he looked.

CHAPTER 8

CAMP

Rusty's head was hanging as they came from the long coulee of the Little Prickly Pear Creek. The sun was hot on his right shoulder as Eli lifted his hat to wipe the sweat from his forehead with his sleeve. The hills had pushed back away from the willow-lined creek, offering a wide grassy bottomed park formed by the confluence of a couple of no-name creeks. But within a short distance, bald hills rose on the right, and a taller hill, thick with timber on the north slope, stood as a bastion to the mouth of another long valley that carried the Little Prickly Pear Creek.

Eli reached down and stroked the stallion's neck as he nudged him to the edge of the creek, "We'll stop for a bit, get some water and maybe a bit of grass, but we'll push on through these hills before we find us a camp for the night. That alright with you, boy?" he asked, as Rusty turned his head back to look at his rider, but as he neared the water, he paid more attention to the clear chuckling stream and before Eli slid down, Rusty already had his nose in the water, with the grey close beside to get his fair share as well.

A big mule deer with velvet-covered antlers spooked from the willows and flashed his white rump with raised tail as he bounded away into a cut between the hills. Rusty lifted his head at the crashing of the willows, but dropped it back for some more of the clear, cold water. Eli waited till the horses backed away to drop the reins and lead rope to ground tie the horses before he knelt to one knee and scooped up a handful of water, always watchful as he drank. With his thirst slaked, he stood in the shade of a tall alder, watched the horses snatch mouthfuls of grass, and looked about at the valley. There were prospect holes scattered on the faces of the hills, but not as many as before. There were no obvious prospect camps within sight, and he seemed to be alone in the mouth of the valley.

Since leaving the stage station at Lyons Creek, the road hugged the hills on the east side of the creek, but shortly after entering the coulee above the park the road crossed the shallow creek at a gravelly bottomed crossing and hung on the steep shoulders on the east side. The north-facing slopes of the hills on the east side of the creek, were thick with timber, spruce, fir, and pine, that gave the slopes an almost black shadow that painted their faces. While on the west side, only two of the north-facing slopes were painted with pine. After a dogleg bend in the creek in the shadow of the longest and steepest timbered face, the hills began to push back away from the little meandering creek and offer a wide, flat valley.

Eli reined up for a quick look around, pointed Rusty to the west flank of the valley aiming for a thickly timbered slope above a small creek. He and the horses were ready for camp and some rest. The sun was touching the horizon and began painting the western sky with a palette of gold, orange, red, and yellow, the bright colors reflecting onto the flats and the hills, painting the landscape with muted shades. The wide flats that stretched to the south and east were carpeted with sage, greasewood, rabbitbrush, and a variety of cacti from yucca to hedgehog, prickly pear and cholla. The dryer flats made the dark green of tall timber more appealing and Rusty quickened his pace, but he stopped with head lifted, nostrils flaring and a slight tremble, just as screams, shouts, and gunfire came from the creek bottom that was thick with willows, alder, and cottonwood.

With one motion, Eli slipped the Winchester from the scabbard under his right leg and dug heels to the big stallion as he pushed toward the creek. This did not sound like a fight among men, but Eli frowned with a scorn, as he listened. When a ground rumbling roar lifted above the greenery, he knew immediately what was happening. He jammed the Winchester back into the scabbard and reined up Rusty, bailed off the saddle and snatched the Spencer from the pack saddle. He jacked a round into the chamber and started toward the ruckus. Screams were still lifting above the willows, thrashing and crashing had overcome any shooting and Eli feared the big bear, probably a grizzly, was getting the best of his prey.

He hugged the willows as his long legs carried him closer. He saw the big bear, standing on his hind legs, pawing at the air, blood on his jowls, and as he cocked his head to the side the big beast opened his mouth wide and let loose a rumbling roar that seemed to shake the very leaves on every nearby tree. A whimper came from the ground as the grizzly snapped his jaws and pawed at the air. Eli took a quick aim, dropped the hammer on the big .52 caliber Spencer, and the rifle bucked, roared, and spat smoke and lead. He quickly jacked another round, brought the hammer to full cock and took another quick aim as the bear swatted at the pesky insect that bit his chest and drew blood. Another bullet from the Spencer painted another red blossom on the upper chest of the bear, striking at the base of the beast's neck, and Eli jacked another round.

The bear dropped to all fours, growling and snapping, as Eli crashed through the willows and splashed across the creek. The bear turned his attention to the distraction, started to rise again, but Eli fired again, the bullet smashing into the cheek of the bear, knocking his head aside, causing the beast to stumble. But he turned toward Eli, shaking his head as if he had been slapped, and lifted a paw, hesitated, and Eli fired again, the bullet blossoming on the neck of the bear, smashing the beast's throat, causing him to stumble, blood spewing from his jaw, mouth, and neck, and fell to one shoulder. He tried to rise to all fours, buried his face in the grass as he pushed with his haunches, his front paws under his chest. Eli jacked another round, cocked the hammer, and fired again, the bullet whistled past the bear's jowls, buried itself in his upper chest and drove him to the ground.

Eli paused, the Spencer ready to fire again, as Eli stood no more than ten feet away, as he watched the bear for any movement, but the grizzly lay still. Eli looked about, saw the body of one mutilated man tucked under the overhang of willows, and another man, trying to move and rise, on the far side of the bear. Eli went to the bear, poked its eye with the muzzle of the Spencer, but the big brown mass did not move. With a tentative step past the bear's muzzle, Eli went to the side of the man that still moved. He looked down at the whiskery-faced man who looked to be in the neighborhood of thirty, obviously a prospector, with a pair of claw marks from his left shoulder to his right hip, blood coming freely from the gashes. The right side of his face had been peeled like a potato, the skin hanging over his ear. The man looked at Eli, "I'm dyin', ain't I?"

"Dunno. I'll see if I can get you bandaged up a little." Eli looked about the camp, saw a rolled-out bedroll at the base of a ponderosa, not far from the creek, and slipped the Spencer over his shoulder with the sling and stepped behind the man, lifted him with hands under his shoulders, and dragged him to the blankets. He grabbed another blanket, went to the creek and ripped it into strips, soaked several of them and returned to clean and bind the wounds. He looked at the man, "I'm gonna try to get the bleeding stopped with bandages, then I'll get some poultices together to doctor you up a little. You just hold still and hang on." A groan came from the still form as he tried to nod but appeared to drop into unconsciousness.

————

IT WAS WELL after sundown before Eli was able to sit back and rest. After dragging the carcass of the bear away from the camp behind a very reluctant Rusty, cutting out all the big claws, and building up the fire, he put some poultices of sage, prickly pear pads, and bee balm on the man's wounds. The man seemed to be resting, and Eli had dug a shallow grave for his partner. Eli leaned against a big rough-barked ponderosa, watching the coffeepot dance beside the fire, and glanced around the camp. Hanging in the tree just away from the camp was the recently skinned carcass of a mule deer. *That's what the bear was after,* mulled Eli, shaking his head. He knew he had to either start smoking that meat, or get it further away from the camp, but he was too tired right now. Maybe after some coffee.

It had taken a while for the horses to settle down after the strong smell of the bear, but they were now grazing in the lower end of the camp, enjoying the lush grass. This had been a good camp, except for their stupidity about fresh meat hanging, and their rocker sat at the edge of the water, but the diggings appeared to be new within the last couple days. He knew that all about this country, there were many camps just like this, also with greenhorns that knew little about the mountains and the ways of the wilderness. But when they are blinded by greed and the lust for gold, everything else becomes unimportant, even to the protecting of their own lives.

He had a passing thought about his boys, wondering if they were with a camp like this. Greenhorns that knew very little about gold and where and how to find it, and absolutely nothing about surviving in a land of blood-thirsty Natives and hungry bears, not to mention the outlaws, hostiles, renegades, and general no-good crowds.

He reached for the coffeepot but a voice from the trees stopped him with, "Hold it right there! Keep your hands where we can see 'em!"

Eli froze in place, squinting toward the black trees and asked, "Who're you?"

"Who're *you*?! This is the claim of friends of our'n. Where're they at?"

"Come out of the trees and I'll show you. One of 'ems layin' over there on his blankets."

The willows pushed aside and two men, both in whipcord britches, hobnail boots, and linen shirts, came into the light of the fire, both holding rifles pointed toward Eli. Eli lifted both hands, nodded to the blankets, "One of 'em is there. I bandaged him up, but he hasn't come around yet. Don't know if he will."

"Whar's the other'n?" growled the bigger of the two.

"Buried him in the trees, yonder," answered Eli, nodding to the trees back from the creek.

"Wha'happened?" whined the second man.

"If you walk o'er yonder past them boulders, you'll see the carcass of a big grizz. That's what happened. Took a half dozen bullets from my Spencer to put him down."

But the bigger of the two men interrupted, "What-samatta, cain't you hit nuttin' wit' that there Spencer?"

"It just takes a bit more to kill a big grizzly. When they stand eight feet tall and weigh more'n a horse, with claws long as your fingers and teeth a long as your thumb, they take a bit of killin'. And then it was all I could do to get my horse," nodding to the two horses who now stood, heads up, ears pricked, looking at the visitors, "to drag that monster away from the camp here. Hard as it was, it was easier'n movin' him," nodding to the man on his blankets.

The two visitors looked at Eli, back to one another, and the big man walked over to the man on the blankets, looked down, turned away and returned to the fire. With a nod to his friend, he sat down on the big rock beside the fire, sat his rifle down and looked at Eli. "I'm Blackie, this here's Shorty. These two was Whispers an' Red.

Don't know their real names, most folks don't use 'em 'round'chere."

Eli lifted the coffeepot to offer the two visitors some of the black brew, "I'm Eli. Eli McCain. I'm not prospectin', but I am lookin' for someone."

Blackie, whose name suited as he had thick coal black hair, whiskers, and his clothes were almost the same color with dirt and grease, growled, "You a lawman?"

Eli chuckled, shook his head, "No, no. I'm looking for my twin sons, Jubal and Joshua Paine. They're supposed to be somewhere hereabouts working for some miner."

"What'chu wan'em fer?"

"Their mother asked for them to come home, so…" he shrugged.

The man nodded, relaxed a little, and poured himself some coffee. He glanced toward the man on the blankets, "Ain't never know'ed a bear to do that. An' he kilt Red huh?"

"Ummhmm. I take it you've never seen a grizzly bear?"

"Nope. Ain't got 'em back in the hills back home in Tennessee. Got black bear, an' they can be mean sometimes, but ain't never seen a grizzly."

"You should take a look at that one come daylight. You'll see how big they are and take a look at the size of their paws and their claws, you'll see how they could easily kill a man."

Shorty piped up, "You gonna take o'er their claim?"

"No. Whispers might still recover and it's his claim. Sides, I am not interested in prospecting."

The two men looked at him with a little suspicion showing in their expressions, but Eli just sipped his coffee and let them think what they would. "You're welcome to camp here, watch over him. That'll let me get on my way and tend to my business."

The men looked at one another, back to Eli. Blackie said, "We just might. They were starting to show color, so we might help 'em out, split the takin's."

CHAPTER 9

PLACER

"How many more ya' reckon we oughta get?" asked Joshua, watching Jubal cut into the tall but skinny lodgepole pine.

"We can snake 'bout four or five of 'em behind each horse an' we got, what, six so far? What with the last two loads, this might be 'nuff," explained Jubal, standing and wiping the sweat off his forehead with his well-used neckerchief. He took a couple deep breaths, picked up the bow saw, and continued working at the tree. They were both on the uphill side of this tree and had been instructed not to clear-cut the trees, to leave the bigger ones and work around them. That suited the brothers, the trees they had been taking were at most eight inches in diameter and when trimmed were no more than ten to twelve feet in length, easy to handle.

"I dunno 'bout you, but I'm thinkin' this is a mite harder than drivin' a freight wagon," grumbled Joshua, sitting on the big rock in the shade of a towering ponderosa.

"Oh, quit your gripin'. What'd you expect—a picnic with the ladies?" Jubal was the stronger of the twins, more dominant and outgoing, but Joshua had been the thinker. Usually choosing to sit back and observe before deciding, while Jubal made the quick decision and took the initiative. "After all, we came here to learn, didn't we?" The creak of the tree and the splintering of the dead branches warned Jubal to step back. He stumbled and fell on his rump just as the trunk cracked and snapped as the tall tree slowly fell down the slope, skidding a short way before coming to a stop.

"Your turn," declared Jubal, stretching out the bow saw to his brother, who slowly rose and accepted the offering as he began looking for another tree to fell.

The brothers stepped off the horses and went to the pole drag, slipped off the rope and began stacking the poles on the ever-growing pile. Below them at the edge of the Prickly Pear Creek, Levi Mallory and Evan Donahue were busy at their rockers, but looked up and waved at the brothers. Joshua looked at his brother as they grabbed the next pole to throw it up on the stack, "I'd rather be learnin' 'bout gold than about timber."

"We will, we will. Levi said we'll start building the flume tomorrow. He said we have to make the flume about five hundred feet, maybe more, alongside the creek to carry water from upstream and wash the gold ore downstream."

"I'm just anxious to get my hands on some gold. They've said they been doin' alright, but they expect the sluice to more than double, maybe triple their take. But I ain't heard him say anything about increasin' our pay any," groused Joshua.

"Oh, quit'cher complainin', it beats gettin' shot at, don't it?" offered Jubal.

"Yeah, I reckon," mumbled the younger brother, as they continued stacking the poles.

————

It was early morning when Levi woke up the brothers. They had stretched out their bedrolls in the edge of the trees, back from the creek and the thickets of willow and alder. The gold camp had a good-sized wall tent used by the two men, complete with a stove for warming and cooking, if need be, but most of the space was taken by their two cots. Jubal and Joshua had made their temporary camp in the trees and when they had time, would make a lean-to shelter for themselves. Levi nudged their feet, "Time to roll out! Got work to do an' coffee's gettin' cold!"

The twins grumbled but tossed aside their blankets and sat up, rubbing sleep from their eyes. A quick glance showed everything the same in the gold camp. Rocker boxes sat side by side at creek's edge, shovels jammed into the gravel bank, and the cookfire blazing with the coffeepot dancing.

Evan Donahue, the other partner, was sitting at the fire tending a big skillet with smoke rising around it as he flipped the strips of sow belly. He had pushed aside the sliced potatoes to keep them hot, as he finished up with the bacon. He looked up at the others, "Come'n git it while it's hot!" He moved the frying pan to the flat rock, grabbed the coffeepot with a rag on the handle, and started pouring the lined-up cups full.

As they sat around in a semi-circle near the fire, absorbing the warmth to dispel the cool air of early morning, Levi began, "I'm gonna show you fellas how to make the racks for the flume while Evan keeps at the rockers. You should get at least a dozen, maybe more, made by midday, then we'll start puttin' things together."

"You mean the flume?" asked Joshua.

Levi nodded as he sipped his coffee, "Ummhmm, the flume'll carry the water down from upstream, and we'll have the sluice, a Long Tom, set up near here'abouts. When it's in place, then we'll be haulin' ore from the hillside back here," pointing behind them at the talus slope, "and wash it out in the sluice."

The first claim sat between the timbered hills and a wagon road of sorts. It straddled the Prickly Pear Creek for a good twelve hundred feet, including the big dogleg bend at the mouth of a coulee, and about two hundred feet on both sides of the creek. The second claim abutted the first and rose up the hill behind them. It was in the face of the bluff they expected to find better veins and with one of the partners having the claim with water, the other having the claim with the vein, they anticipated doing very well with their gold work.

It was just off the Prickly Pear Creek, further into the valley below them, that the original Last Chance Gulch strike was made, just over two years ago. Now the creek, the hillsides, the flats, were all crawling with prospectors, miners, gold seekers of every age, origin, and color. What had been a wilderness just three years ago, the few searchers came north from Alder Gulch, Bannack, and Virginia City when the placers started playing out or had all been taken, and the overflow had come to Last Chance Gulch. But now there were towns springing up everywhere. Just downstream from this claim, Montana City was beginning to grow, and further into the valley, the bigger settlement of Helena was blossoming into a real town.

"After you get the racks or braces made, we'll start on the flume. We got that lumber in town and that barrel of tar there, we'll use for sealing the flume, but that'll come later. Soon's you get done eatin', we'll get started," he nodded to the stack of poles.

————

By noon, the twins had eighteen H-braces made, and the other poles trimmed, cut to length, and ready to assemble. Levi walked up the slight slope to the stack of braces, looked at the completed frames and smiled, nodding. "Good work. Let's go get us somethin' to eat an' then we'll get started on the flume boxes."

The twins went to the creek, stripped off their shirts and splashed water on themselves, both to cool off and clean up a little. They walked back to the fire, doing up their shirts and tucking in the tails as Evan grinned up from the pot of stew, and said, "It's ready! Hope you're hungry, cuz I made a big pot. What you don't eat now, we'll heat up for supper!"

Jubal and Joshua looked at one another, grinned, and shook their heads as they bent to reach for the plates and fill them with the offered vittles. With steaming coffee in hand, they took the same seats they used in the morning and began to devour the offerings. Levi and Evan talked with each other, but the boys were near and easily heard. "What'dya figger we got this mornin'? An ounce, two, more?" asked Levi. He had been at the rocker less than Evan.

Evan grinned, reached in his shirt pocket, and pulled out a nugget the size of his thumbnail, "Not countin' this," as he handed it to Levi, "we got close to two ounces."

Levi turned the nugget over and over in his fingers, shaking his head and grinning. "That's a beaut! Close to an ounce, mebbe more!"

"It's just over two ounces!" declared a grinning Evan, accepting the nugget back from his partner.

Jubal and Joshua looked at one another, wide-eyed and grinning. Joshua spoke softly, "That's four ounces at fourteen dollars an ounce! That's more'n what most make in a month!"

Evan and Levi heard the exclamation and Evan added, "Close! And that's only a half-day. But not all days yield a nice nugget like that. We're hopin' when we get the Long-Tom up, we'll do maybe three times that every day!"

"And what do we make?" asked Joshua, wide-eyed and hopeful.

Evan looked at Levi and back to the twins, "The more we make, the more you make!" he declared, smiling. "It won't be a full share, but it'll be good, we promise. The harder you work, the more we make, the more you'll get."

The brothers looked at one another, grinning and chuckling, until Jubal said, "Let's get to building that sluice!"

CHAPTER 10

HELENA

E li sat in the saddle, forearms crossed atop the saddle horn, reins dangling from his left hand, as he looked out over the wide expanse of the valley. He was on a bald knob that overlooked the valley he estimated to be about ten miles across and twelve or thirteen miles north to south. After leaving the camp of the prospectors where the grizzly had wreaked havoc, and they buried the man known as Whispers, he had followed Silver Creek through the last few hills and now sat atop the lowest of the bald knobs that stair-stepped to a higher timber-topped hill to the south. The short stretch of Silver Creek saw its share of placer miners on the creek, busy at their pans and rockers, and the usual pockmarked hills made unsightly by the many prospect holes.

The valley was a beehive of activity, and it looked like most of the building of the town was on the south end of the valley in the shadow of what he would later learn was Mount Helena, but the grassy flats were also dimpled with wall tents, miner's shacks, tipis and more.

A weathered tipple stood over a mine shaft that had been sunk in the shoulder of the hill to the southeast of town. Several other mines showed headframes and tipples that dotted the countryside and each with several workers busy round about. He noticed every working claim that sat on the creek, the men were busy, but vigilant, always with rifles nearby as they watched Eli ride past. One man was usually within quick reach of a rifle or stood with a rifle in hand. None were friendly and Eli hastened past, intent on making his inquiries in the town and at any of the larger claims or working mines.

He nudged Rusty off the knob, leaned back in the saddle over the cantle to counterbalance the big stallion's toe digging descent of the hillside. When they dropped onto the flat, Eli relaxed in the seat, looking around to take in all the activity. Greenery that bounded a creek snaked its way across the broad valley bottom, often obscured by the many wall tents and shacks of gold hunters using the gravelly waterways to pan for gold. The wagon road he followed sided the hills on the west edge of the valley, and wherever he looked, prospect holes with the apron of dug out dirt, marred the beauty of God's creation. He shook his head, grinned, and pushed on toward the town.

Although the hills on his right swept back to show a sweep of dry land blanketed with sage, greasewood, and rabbitbrush, the road crossed the creek on a reinforced log bridge, built to carry heavy ore wagons. A small sign identified the waterway as Ten Mile Creek and once across, another sign at a junction pointed travelers to Kessler Brewery upstream of the crossing. Eli grinned, mumbled to himself, *Must be growing to have their own brewery*.

As he rode into the bustling town, the streets were

crowded with wagons, buggies, horses, and many, many people, all of whom looked somewhat alike with canvas britches, linen shirts, hobnail boots, and usually some semblance or piece of either a Union or Confederate uniform. The buildings were mostly clapboard, most with false fronts, but a few were rising above the rest with brick facades. He spotted a two-story building with big lettering *Paynes Hotel* with a balcony overhanging the boardwalk and several men standing at the rail, watching the busy streets below.

He slapped the reins around the hitchrail, grabbed the lead rope of the packhorse and slipped it over the hitchrail and stepped onto the boardwalk. He paused, looking around at the strange sight of so many buildings, all no more than two or three years old, with false fronts, hanging signs, boardwalks, all overlooking a churned up muddy street. Even though there had not been any significant rain in several days, the sloppy streets were made so by thrown out wastewater, emptied thunder buckets, and any other waste. There was a bitter stench to the town, made so by the mix of gunpowder, vomit, smoke from poorly ventilated cookstoves, unwashed bodies, and everything else that stunk. He shook his head as he turned to enter the hotel, remembering the smell of saltwater at his boyhood home near the ship-builders, where the winds off the ocean carried away the offensive stench of civilization.

A thin man with a cotton shirt and string tie, grinned broadly as Eli neared the front desk. The man's hair was parted down the middle and held flat by some grease that made it shine and the broad smile of the young man seemed genuine. "Welcome, sir, would you like a room?"

"I would, yes. And if you have the facilities for a bath, that would be appreciated also."

The young man frowned, "A bath, sir?" he asked, appearing a little baffled.

"Yes, a bath."

"Whatever for, sir?"

"Haven't you ever had someone ask for a bath before?" asked Eli.

"Uh, no sir. But I've only been working here a few weeks. But no one has asked for a bath before?"

"Haven't you ever had a bath?" asked Eli, somewhat skeptically as he stepped back a bit from the counter and the young man. It had become obvious the young man was not one to bathe regularly, if at all.

The young man smiled, nodding, "Of course, sir. My mother used to make all us boys go down to the crick ever New Year's Day. Sometimes we even had to break the ice, but we done it, real reg'lar."

"Well, if the hotel does not offer baths, is there a bathhouse in town?"

The young man nodded, smiling, "Oh, yes sir. The Chinee have a bathhouse, just down the street, thataway, right next to the blacksmith."

"And a place to put up my horses and gear?"

"Oh, right acrost the street, yonder," he pointed to the front door, "that corral an' tack shed is part of the hotel. You can put yore horses in there, and the gear in the shed."

"What's to keep anyone from stealing my gear?"

The young man frowned, "Stealing? Why would anyone steal yore gear?"

Eli dropped his eyes to the register, and asked, "Does the blacksmith have a livery where he keeps horses and such?"

"Yessir, but you have to pay for that."

"Fine, just sign me in to a room, give me the key, and

I'll go take care of my horses."

————

He left his bedroll and saddlebags in the room, slipped his Winchester in the scabbard under the bed, and after dusting himself off a mite, he went downstairs and out the front door, bound for the bathhouse and livery. It was just a short ways, but in between the hotel and the livery were a half dozen buildings, three of them taverns. But the livery and bathhouse were across the street and Eli drew up in the big door of the livery, stepped down and saw the glow of hot coals as a big man pumped the billows with his foot and worked at a big horseshoe that glowed orange hot.

The big man looked up, took his foot off the billows, and wiped the sweat off his brow as he grinned at Eli. "What'chu need, friend?"

"Need a place to put my horses up, maybe have you check their shoes, take care of 'em for me."

"I can do that. If you ain't in no hurry, go 'head on and put 'em in the empty stalls back yonder," as he waved his hand over his shoulder, "and I'll take a look at 'em later, after I get done wit' these shoes." He leaned to the side to look at the horses, "Cost'chu a buck a day for the two of 'em, includes hay, some grain, an' I'll look at their feet an' let'chu know 'bout the shoein'."

Eli nodded, started to the shady interior of the big barn and soon put the horses into adjoining stalls, stripped the gear and stacked it, forked some hay into the mow and shut the stall gate. He spotted the tack room and made a couple trips to stow his gear in the room. He returned to the smithy and handed him a five-dollar gold coin. "I've got a room at Paynes Hotel."

The smithy nodded, slipped the coin into his pants pocket as Eli continued, "Is there a place nearby where I can get me some clothes?"

"Anything special?"

"No, just another shirt, maybe some britches."

"There's a haber somethin' just the other side of the Chinee bathhouse.

"A haberdashery?"

The smithy grinned, nodded, "Yup, that's it." He frowned, "Why can't they just say it's a store for clothes?"

Eli chuckled, "I dunno, maybe that way they think they can charge more for their stuff."

The big smithy grunted, wiped his meaty paws on his blackened apron, and turned back to his forge.

Eli looked through the windows of the bathhouse but could see nothing in the dark interior. He stepped inside and was welcomed by a grey-haired Chinese woman attired in an embroidered silk kimono. She bowed, nodding, and smiled at Eli, "You want a bath, yes?"

"Yes, but first I need to go next door and get some fresh clothes. Is there a laundry nearby that can take care of these?" he asked, pulling at his linen shirt to indicate the clothes he wore.

"Yes, yes. We do that."

"And what is the cost of a bath?"

"Half-dollar," she replied, nodding and smiling.

"Fresh hot water?"

"One dollar."

"So, if I want clean, fresh, hot water, it costs more?"

"Yes. More work. Must haul water, heat water. Cost more."

He dug a coin from his pocket, handed it to her, "I'll be back. You can get the bath ready for me, alright?"

"Yes, yes. It will be ready."

The haberdashery was well supplied, and it was easy for Eli to pick out a striped hickory shirt, a pair of the new blue denim trousers that were popular with working men, and some drawers and socks. As the clerk, a young woman in a gingham dress and a broad smile under golden locks, tallied up the sale, Eli asked, "I'm looking for someone and I thought you might have seen them here in the store."

"Oh?" replied the clerk, looking up at Eli.

"Two young men, twins," as he spoke, he pulled the tintype from his pocket to show the young lady, "they're my sons. Jubal and Joshua Paine. They were coming here to work for some miner, but I don't know who or where."

She looked at the picture, smiled, "They're good-looking boys," and with another glance to the tintype, "but I don't remember seeing them. Is there some place I can send word if they do show up?"

"Well, I'll be staying at the Paynes Hotel for a few days. I'll be out looking for them."

"You have quite a task before you. This town has been growing so fast, men have been coming in by the hundreds every week, and there has been a lot of violence. Why, just last week, the vigilantes hung another man from the hanging tree."

Eli frowned, "Vigilantes?"

"Yes, that's the only law we have if you want to call it that. They have hung four or five so far this year." She shook her head as she wrapped the new clothes in a bundle of paper and string. She pushed the coins that made up Eli's change across the counter, and smiled, "I hope you find them."

"Thank you," replied Eli as he picked up the parcel and started for the bathhouse.

CHAPTER 11

PROPOSITION

"I'm looking for a friend of mine, he's putting in an emporium and I was told his business was in the same building as a bank. Would you happen to know where that might be?" asked Eli, standing before the front desk in the Paynes Hotel.

The young man that had first greeted him had been replaced by a matronly woman that continually fanned herself and oft used the fan to swat at flies. She raised one eyebrow as she looked at Eli, and asked, "And just what might be the name of this businessman you seek?"

"Martine Beaumont, and his wife is Amélie."

The woman let a hint of a smile touch her face but not her eyes as she answered, "Oh yes, the Frenchies. What are they putting in, something from Paris no doubt?"

"No, just an emporium. They are second generation Americans, although they do speak French. Good people, and I'm sure their store will be an asset to the community," lauded Eli, knowing this woman, like so many others, were judgmental of anyone that was different or might be a threat to their own business.

"I believe their *business* is in the same building as the S.T. Hauser Bank. It is on Main Street, or Last Chance Gulch, and the corner of Sixth. It's just a little ways," she pointed to the northeast.

"Thank you," answered Eli, tipping his hat to the woman and turning on his heel to go to the Beaumonts' store.

The bank building was one of the newer brick buildings, two stories, big windows, and the ground floor was divided, each side with its own entrance. Outside the storefront, a man was standing on a crude ladder, painting a long sign that was flat against the building, but covered the entire length. Most of the sign was painted and said, *Emporium* in large letters, with a secondary line below—*Mining supplies, clothes, hardware, guns.* As Eli drew near, he saw the man on the ladder was Martine and standing below, holding a can of paint, was his wife, Amélie. Eli stood watching for a moment, stepped closer, and asked, "You open yet?"

Martine turned to look, recognized Eli, and declared, "For you, my friend, we will always be open!" and started down from the ladder. His smiling wife offered him a cloth to wipe his hands and he stepped forward to shake hands with Eli. "Come in, come in. We are open, but just not too busy yet. We need more stock, but we can accommodate most."

"Don't let me take you away from your work," offered Eli, leaning back to look up at the sign.

"Oh no, I was just doing a little touch up. It's fine, fine. Come in," he repeated, motioning Eli to the door. As Eli stepped through, Martine grabbed the ladder and brought it inside.

Eli paused, letting his eyes get used to the dim interior, but smiled as he looked around. "Well, I see you do have some stock, but there are a few empty shelves and tables. Have you heard anything about your shipment?"

"Nothing yet, but we're hopeful," answered Martine, walking around the end of the counter to take his place behind the main counter. Amélie grabbed a soft cloth and began dusting the shelves and more as the men talked. Eli and Martine talked for a while, Eli answering questions about his sons, Martine about the stock. As they visited, Martine nodded when two men came through the door and began looking about. One was about the same size as Eli, but shaggy hair protruded from under his felt hat, nervous bug eyes under thick eyebrows took in everything and everyone in the store. He had a dirty buckskin jacket, whipcord trousers, and hobnail boots. The second man was about half a head shorter and fifty pounds lighter, a Monmouth or knit cap that smacked of a deckhand, a canvas jacket that was ragged at the sleeves, and greasy and dirty canvas britches that were tucked in the high-topped boots. Eli stepped back and began fingering some leather goods, casually watching the newcomers without showing his interest.

The bigger man stepped closer to the counter, looked at Martine, "Looks like you got some empty shelves."

Martine nodded, "For now, but we are expecting a shipment soon. Then we'll be well stocked."

"That right? Hmmm," began the big man, looking about, seeing Eli with his back turned, and turned back to Martine, lowered his voice, "I might be able to help you with that."

Martine frowned, "How might *you* be able to help?"

"Wal, we got us three wagons loaded with stock for

just this hyar kinda store. All new stock, just came up the river on the packet *Bertrand*. Seems they had some problem an' had to dump their cargo so they could make it off the sandbar to get back home. And we got it. So, if'n you'd like to get that there cargo, we might work out a deal."

Martine glanced to see Eli coming a little closer, and Martine asked, "What kind of deal?"

Eli had walked near the window to look at the horses the men had tethered out front and spotted a sorrel with two front stockings and a blood bay. He was not certain, but he thought they were two of the horses ridden by the freight thieves. He moved closer to the counter and listened as he hefted a gold pan and examined it carefully.

Martine leaned on the counter, which put him closer to the man, and repeated, "What kind of deal?"

The man chuckled, stood up and looked about, saw the man examining the gold pans, and turned back to the merchant. He reached for a stub of a pencil and a piece of paper and wrote "$2,000." He pushed the paper across the counter and grinned as Martine looked wide-eyed at the figure. The man spoke softly, "Half now, half when we bring it."

Martine looked at the man, glanced over his shoulder at Eli, and said, "I'll have to talk to my partner." He spoke louder, "Say partner, can we talk?" as he motioned to Eli.

Eli nodded, came closer and Martine motioned for them to go to the door to the storeroom and they stepped through. Once inside the room, Martine showed Eli the paper and said, "I don't have that! I paid for my shipment and have very little cash left and what I do have is in the bank. Besides, that's *my* shipment! It was on the *Bertrand*."

"I guessed as much. I saw them unload the boat. I think they told the captain they were the freight company sent to pick up the cargo. They killed the real freighters, burnt a couple of their wagons but probably stole the paperwork they gave to the captain. Look, here's what we'll do…" and he began to lay out a plan that had been formulating in his mind ever since he left the farm where the wagons were stored in the barn. After he finished explaining, Eli looked at Martine, "Is that alright? You understand what needs to be done?"

"Yes, but what about the money they want now?"

"You'll have to convince them you don't have it now but can get it from the bank in a couple days. It will take them three, maybe four days to get here with the wagons."

"I know they'll want something, but all my cash is…" he shrugged.

Eli nodded, pulled a pouch from his waistband, and dropped ten twenty-dollar gold pieces into Martine's hand, and said, "Try to get by with just a hundred dollars. Put half that in one pocket, the rest in the other."

Martine grinned, nodding, and started back through the door. As he pushed open the door, he was surprised when he heard a slap and his wife shout, "Get away from me! Take your hands off me!" Martine slammed open the door to see the second man with one hand on Amélie's shoulder, the other grasping her chin trying to force a kiss, only to receive another slap. She turned, wide-eyed and scared, and Martine rushed toward them, but Eli stopped him as he stepped in front and barked, "Get your hands off that woman now!"

The man turned, grinning, reaching for the butt of a pistol that was in his waistband, but when he looked back at Eli he was staring at the big hole in the muzzle of Eli's Colt, "That's the second stupid stunt you've tried. Go ahead and pull that hogleg, but only if you want to die here and now!" growled Eli.

"Uh, uh…" stammered the knit cap who froze in place and slowly stretched both hands wide to the side, big eyes blinking as he stepped back, glancing to the door and his friend, "I din't mean nuttin', I was just funnin', only wanted a little kiss!" he whimpered.

"That's not the way we treat women here. Take your funnin' out the door, NOW!" demanded Eli, glancing from the one to the other. The Colt was in his right hand, but his left was behind his back, under his vest, and gripped the LeMat pistol. The man looked to his partner, who nodded, and turned to the door. Eli watched until he was outside, then turned to face the bigger man, who stood with hands to the side, "Whoa now, I ain't doin' nuthin', just wanna make a deal here."

Eli slowly nodded and returned his Colt to his holster that sat on his left hip. It was a habit he acquired when in the army, carrying his pistol in the flapped army holster, but where most had it at their right side, Eli preferred it butt forward, but on his left hip and without a flap. When his pistol was stowed, he walked toward the man as Martine looked across the counter. Martine said, "We want the cargo. And we'll pay the two thousand, but we only have one hundred dollars now. We'll have the rest from the bank when you return with the wagons."

The man drew back, looked from Martine to Eli, and said, "Nope. Gotta have more!"

Martine looked to Eli, back to the man, "Alright. Two

hundred, but that's all. We don't know you, so how can we trust you with more? Besides, that is all the cash we have. But we'll have the rest when you return."

The big man looked from one to the other, then stepped closer to reach for the gold coin. But Martine put his hand over the stack, "Not until you sign for this and the shipment."

"Sign? What'chu mean?"

"A receipt to show we paid you this money. And a promise from you to deliver the rest of the goods."

"Oh, yeah, sure. I'll sign." He watched as Martine scratched out the figures on the paper, turned it to face the man and pointed to a line for him to sign. The man looked at it, looked up at Martine, then took the pencil stub and signed on the line, but his signature was a crude printing of *Jones*. "Now, gimme the money!" he demanded.

Martine pushed the stack of coins toward the man who anxiously scooped them up and put them in his pocket. He looked at Martine with a broad grin, "We'll be back in four days with the wagons. You have the rest of the money ready!"

"We will, we will," answered Martine, who glanced to Eli, and back to the back of the man as he exited the store.

Martine looked to Eli, "I sure hope they come back with the goods, I don't want to lose your money!"

"Oh, I won't lose any money. I'm going to trail them even though I'm certain of where they are camped anyway," explained Eli.

They watched the two men mount up and ride away as the door opened again and a man came in, walked straight to the counter, and looked from Eli to Martine, "Those men that were just in here, who are they?"

Eli frowned at the man, "Why do you ask?"

The man glared at Eli, "I'm John X. Beidler, most just call me 'X.' We got word there's some outlaws that have been stealing cargo from packet ships, holding up stage-coaches and freighters, and more. Someone pointed out those two men and thought they were suspicious."

"Are you the law?" asked Eli.

Martine spoke up, "No, he's not the law, Eli. But he is a friend and...well, we do have a sheriff, George Wood, but..." he looked at Beidler, back to Eli, "the only real law here in Helena is the Committee of Safety or what most call vigilantes."

Eli looked at Beidler. He was not a big man, maybe six inches over five feet, a stocky build, long sideburns, and a bushy drooping moustache. But he had piercing black eyes and his flat brimmed peaked hat hid his bald dome that was evident when he pushed the hat back on his head. Eli asked, "Are you one of the vigilantes?"

"I don't know who the vigilantes are, but, well, I do know how to get word to them. Now tell me about those men."

CHAPTER 12

VIGILANTES

"When the gold started to peter out in Alder Gulch, many of us came here to Last Chance Gulch. There had been several good finds and, well, we thought we'd give it a try. There were several of us that knew the workings of the vigilantes in Alder Gulch country, Wilbur Sanders, Anton Holder, and a few others, so when things were getting out of hand, we thought it would be good to try to put things together. We talked to several others, told what we knew about the way things worked down south, and we decided we'd have a Committee of Safety.

"So, after the territory was formed, the powers that be formed three judicial districts. This one is the Third District, Helena and all the surrounding settlements. We got our first chief judge last August, Judge Lyman Munson. But he hasn't been much help, although he has not interfered nor made any attempt to stop the Committee."

"What's been done so far, I mean, regarding enforcing the law?" asked Eli.

"Well, last June, there was a shooting, and we had a community trial, found a fella name of John Keene guilty of killin' a man name of Harry Slater. Shot him in the head in a saloon. So, he was taken out to the old Hangman's Tree and strung up.

"After that they caught a Jack Silvie, a known road agent, and 'fore he was hung, he confessed to bein' a member of a band of road agents that had committed at least a dozen murders. He decorated that same Hangman's Tree." Beidler leaned back against a table that was stacked with shirts, crossed his arms, and looked at Eli and Martine. "That's 'bout the lay of things."

"Well, let me tell you about those men," began Eli, nodding to the door to indicate the two who had ridden out. "When I first saw them, they had two wagons and a surly attitude. But…" he continued to explain about the riverboat cargo, the burned wagons and bodies, and where the wagons were stashed at the farm. "But I had no proof, and I was pretty well outnumbered, so I thought I'd just come into town, see if they showed up, and…" he shrugged.

He continued, "What I suggested to Martine, was to get them to bring the wagons into town, then, well, I hadn't got that far with the planning. But now that you're here, and can talk to the vigilantes…" but he was interrupted by Beidler, "Committee of Safety."

"Well, I never was much of one for committees. My dad used to say that a camel was a horse put together by a committee." He shook his head, leaned on the counter, "The way I see it, we can hit 'em at the farm, but I don't know about the family there, *or* along the Benton Road somewhere, *or* wait till they get into town, and we can take 'em here."

Beidler looked from Eli to Martine, "I'll talk to the

others, I think this is the same outfit we've run into before and if it is, they're trouble. I'm not the one that calls the shots, it's kind of a majority rule, so..." he shrugged.

Eli nodded, "I'm concerned about the family at the farm. There were at least two women, but I couldn't tell about kids or any others. And if this bunch doesn't think anything about killing and burning like they did the freighters, those women might be in danger. I'm gonna leave things in your hands about the wagons and such, I'm gonna try to get back to that farm and see if I can help those folks."

"What if they're a part of the gang?" asked Martine.

"Dunno, I'll just have to try to figger that out," resolved Eli.

———

THE BIG STALLION liked to stretch out. He had a ground-eating canter that was smooth and easy. With the dapple grey back at the livery, he could move at his own pace, and he stretched out his long legs to put the crowded valley of the Last Chance Gulch behind them. He was on a different trail, suggested by Beidler, that should save him at least half a day. Beidler had said, "It cuts through the hills, then takes the far side of the Bear Tooth, what some are calling the Sleeping Giant, drops down near the river and stays closer to the river, and if you want, you can cross over and there's an easy trail on the south side of the river. But further on, the Benton Road is about the best."

When he dropped out of the rugged hills, he had a bit of a reprieve for about eight miles before the road followed the Big Muddy through the hills that were strewn with basaltic formations, rocky outcroppings, and limestone configurations and peppered with the tough piñon that burrowed into the cracks of rocks to take root and hold on to grow where nothing else could. It was rugged country, tough, hot, and even the Big Muddy had to give way to the rocky hills. The road was good, and he rode into the night, the big moon was waxing full and cast a muted blue light that seemed to dance among the rocks and trees.

But when Rusty started slowing his pace, they were just about to break out into the flats and Eli spotted a ridge to his left, north of the river, that looked like the Creator had gathered a handful of basaltic slabs and stacked them against the face of the hills. A break in the rock offered some shelter and cover and he pointed Rusty into the cut, saw an overhang on the back side of the ridge and some greenery that indicated water, and pulled up, stepped down, and led Rusty to the water. While the horse drank, Eli loosened the girth, bent for a drink himself, and returned to the overhang. They were protected from sight by a tall growth of buckbrush, and with Rusty tethered within reach of some grass, Eli rolled out his blankets and was soon asleep, trusting Rusty to warn him of any danger.

————

THE THIN LINE of grey showed above the eastern horizon as Eli rode from the canyon of the Missouri. He knew he was still about fifteen miles from the farm where the wagons were hidden, but he also did not want to show himself to anyone from the gang. What many think is flat land, is usually rolling with swells and dips that could hide an entire war party as well as a gang of eight outlaws with three wagons, but for all he knew, they were still at the farm and that was what he was counting on. But he still showed caution, keeping to the low dips and using any natural cover to hide his approach.

It was mid-afternoon when he recognized the road that split off the Mullan Road and hugged the south edge of the wide, grassy flat, making its way to the peninsula tip of the wide bend in the river. He left the road and kept to the cottonwoods and willows that marked the river, ever watchful of any other riders or lookouts that would spot his approach. He saw a thin tendril of smoke beyond the low hill he used before and nudged Rusty into the trees. A quick glance to the sky told him he had at least a couple hours of daylight left, but he was not anxious to try to get to the farmhouse before dark. Although the farm buildings were near the point of land, they were still away from the trees, and it would be diffi-cult to get near in the daylight.

With binoculars hanging from his neck, Winchester in hand, he started through the tall grass to the crest of the hill. He bellied down at the crest and crawled to the point for his look-see. He took a careful scan, not just of the farm buildings, but also the trees where he remembered the rest of the gang had camped. There was no activity at the farm, neither the house nor the barn showed movement. A couple of cows stood chewing their cuds and swishing their tails as they basked in the late afternoon sun. Several horses were standing hipshot in the corral, mules sought shade in the fenced field, and a lazy dog was stretched out on the porch. The curtains in the farmhouse moved, but that could have been from the breeze through the open door. And the camp in the trees had no activity. It was a tranquil scene that belied the evil that was hidden within.

Eli lowered the field glasses, wondering about the lack of movement. Surely, they had not all left, the barn doors were closed, and the mules were still there. There was a little smoke coming from the chimney, probably the kitchen stove. He lifted the glasses again, focused on the house and waited, watching the windows and the open door. He started to move the glasses to the barn, but movement stopped him. The big figure of the bully boss stepped into the doorway, leaning against the door-jamb, and looking toward the trees. He pulled a pouch from his pocket and began to roll a cigarette, filled the paper with tobacco, replaced the pouch in his pocket, and lifted the paper to his mouth to lick the paper and seal the roll. He was speaking to someone inside the house as he put the cigarette in his lips and pulled a lucifer from his pocket, lit the match and then his cigarette. He inhaled deeply, stepped out onto the porch, and pulled the rocking chair away from the wall and seated himself.

When the big man leaned forward, looking down the road, and stood to shade his eyes and look, Eli turned back to look at the road. Four riders were coming toward the house, and he lifted the binoculars for a better look. The two in the lead were the same two that had come into the store and Eli let a grin split his face, knowing he was right about his assumptions that they were a part of this same gang. But with four riders, one man in the house, that meant there were at least three others some-where. He had to know where they were before he could do anything. He had been thinking out a way to make it through the trees, come onto the house from behind, and maybe see if the farmer and his women were there and if they were part of this gang.

The riders stopped in front of the house, stepped down and were greeted by the big man that Eli had identified as the boss of the bunch. It was a friendly greeting, hand shaking, back slapping, laughter and more, until the boss sent the four to the barn to put away their horses and go to their camp. He went back into the house, slamming the door behind him. Eli watched the others and when they slid open the big door of the barn, he spotted the wagons inside.

Within moments, the four men walked to the trees to their camp, but Eli did not see any of the others. He shook his head, looked at the sun slowly nearing the western horizon, and wondered about the others. He knew he couldn't wait until morning to find out about the family, but he was hesitant to try to approach the cabin, only to find out the others were on watch. *Last time, there were a couple in the barn, taking care of the animals. Maybe they're still there and the other one is in the house with the big boss.* He knew it would be a gamble, but what wasn't, and the safety of those women might be dependent on what he does before this bunch of outlaws left with the wagons. If they do the same as with the freighters, they would leave no one alive.

CHAPTER 13

DISCOVERY

K arl Fischer, the number two man of the gang led by Ludvik Kowalski, started barking orders to the three men as they entered the barn. "Jonesy, you and Lloyd start gatherin' the mules, Gunnie, you and me will gather up the harness."

"You mean to say we're really gonna hitch 'em up tonight? We gonna let 'em stand or what?" grumbled Jonesy, frowning at Karl and glancing to his partner, Lloyd.

"That's right. I knew that's what he'd do, the moon's full, an' we need to make time while we can. The sooner we get to town the sooner we get our money!" answered Karl, motioning for the two to get to the field and drive the mules back to the barn.

Jonesy looked to Lloyd, shaking his head as he motioned to his partner to come along. When they were out of range of hearing, Lloyd said, "You know, I was thinkin' we shoulda just split that two hunnert dollars an' left the country. A hunnert dollars can last me a good long time an' I'm thinkin' we're headin' into a peck o' trouble with these two."

"Yeah, but if we stick around, we'll both have two hunnert dollars an' that'll last a bit longer. Then if'n we want, we can take off on our own," answered Jonesy.

"What'chu think he's gonna do with those wimmen?" asked Lloyd.

"You still worried 'bout them? Huh. He'll prob'ly just leave 'em tied up till we git gone. That way, it'll take a while and we'll be long gone an' if'n they're smart, they'll be glad to see us go and leave things alone," surmised Jonesy as he motioned to Lloyd to swing wide and drive the bunch of mules back toward the barn.

While Jonesy and Lloyd went after the mules, Karl sent Gunnie after the other men at the camp. When the others returned, Karl growled at the others, "Antonio, Clark, Lewis, you three help Jonesy and Lloyd get the mules harnessed and hooked up, pull the wagons outta the barn, then catch up the horses and get them saddled and geared up. We're pullin' out soon."

Antonio Rodriguez frowned, "We're leaving in the dark? Why we do such a thing?"

Karl shook his head and frowned at the one the others called the Mex, "We're leaving so we can get closer to the town. Then we'll make camp, get some sleep, have some breakfast, and make it into town 'fore it's too late. And you," nodding to Antonio, "soon's you finish with the harnessin', you come to the house."

"Si, si. I come," grinned the wiry man, knowing that whenever the boss sent for him it usually meant he had a job for his particular skills, especially with his knives. Antonio chuckled as he fingered the haft of the knife at his hip, and turned back to the harnessing, anxious for his next job.

WITH ALL THE activity around the barn, Eli guessed
they were getting ready to leave with the wagons, but he
had to get to the farmhouse and the family within. With
one last scan in the dim light with his binoculars, he
replaced them in the case and crabbed back through the
grass to the bottom of the knoll. Once out of sight of the
house and barn, he went to a crouch and moved into the
trees where Rusty was picketed. He replaced the rifle in
the scabbard, slipped his high-topped moccasins from
the saddlebags, and stroked the horse's neck and spoke
softly, "You just sit tight, boy, enjoy the grass, and if
everything goes well, I'll be back in a little bit." With his
moccasins on, he checked the loads in his Colt and
LeMat pistols, felt his Bowie knife that hung in a sheath
between his shoulder blades, and satisfied, took a deep
breath and muttered a short prayer. He checked the
reins, knew the horse would stay ground tied, but could
move about for graze and water, if need be, and with a
last stroke of the big stallion's neck, he started toward
the riverbank. He had mentally mapped out the route he
would take to the house, wanting to come up at the back,
using the darkness and the brush near the house to mask
his approach, but for a short stretch, he would be visible
from the barn.

As he moved through the underbrush at the edge of
the riverbank, Eli remembered his time with the Crow
scout, *Ischu Shi Dish*, or Half Yellow Face, who had been a
friend when he was serving at Fort Laramie. The two
young men had spent a lot of time together, learning
about the culture of their people and the ways of the
warriors. Half Yellow Face had taught Eli the ways of
stalking game or an enemy, how to move silently and

unseen through the brush and woods. Half Yellow Face had said he would have been a good Crow warrior, if he wasn't a stupid white man. Eli chuckled at the memory, but naturally applied all he had learned as he slowly worked his way closer to the house.

There was no light at the rear of the house, but a shaft of yellow fell from a window on the near side, the far side faced the barn, and the front of the house faced the road. Eli slipped closer, stepped into the dark shadow at the back and paused, listening and watching for any movement within the house, or close by coming from the barn. Muffled talk came from within, but he only heard one voice, until the slap of the screen door told of another coming into the house.

Eli inched around the corner of the house, closer to the window with the light. Voices came through the open window. What he recognized as the bully boss, said, "We're gonna be leavin' so we're tyin' you up and that'll give us time to get away. If you're smart, you won't get in no hurry to get loose an' when you do, you best just stay here and keep yore mouths shut. You ain't been no trouble, so, we'll just leave you tied and gagged. Shouldn't take you too long to get loose, unnerstand?"

Eli heard the response of a man, probably the farmer, "Yeah, just go easy on the women. I'll keep 'em here and you can go your way."

Eli moved a little closer to look through the window. A man sat in a chair, his hands tied behind his back, two women sat side by side at the table, standing before them was the man Eli had talked to before, the bully boss, Ludvik Kowalski, and beside him two others. One man that was dressed like a Mexican vaquero with a bolero jacket, flared trousers, both decorated with ornate stitching, stood grinning and fingering a knife with inlaid silver in the haft, and another man that glared at the farmer while the boss man talked, occasionally nodding his agreement with what the big man said. When the big man motioned to the others to step outside to the porch, Eli moved along the side of the house, ducking low to miss the light from the window, and stood near the corner, to listen to the men.

Vik spoke softer, but his gravelly voice was easily heard. "Karl, I want you to get one of the others to stay here with the Mex. And you," obviously turning his attention to the small man, "you do your thing. But give us some time to get further down the road, I don't want anyone hearing what's happening. They'll be tied up so you can do what you want, then set the house afire, but like I said, wait till we're long gone."

"Si, si. I unnerstand. I weel do what you want. Hehe-hehe," cackled the smaller man. What Eli could not see was the man fingering the blade of his knife, grinning ear to ear.

Eli moved back into the shadows, looking all about, wanting to know the house better, any windows, doors, or anything that would make noise and give away his presence. He moved away from the house and dropped to his haunches amid the brush, thinking about what and how he would do, for he knew he could not just watch these people murdered.

It was just a short while when he heard the crack of bullwhips and the rattle of trace chains, and he knew the wagons were on the move. He let the sounds of the wagons mask his movements as he moved back to the house. With a quick look in the window, he went to the back door, and slowly pushed it open. There was no direct light in the back room which he could tell was the kitchen area, and he stepped inside, pulling the door shut quietly behind him as he moved away from the doorway to step into the corner, letting the darkness fold around him. He remembered seeing a dog on the front porch, and hoped it was still on the porch or at least away from the house, although he was not too concerned about the dog for it had showed no alarm about any of the other men.

He waited in the stillness, the thin curtain at the doorway hiding his presence. In the next room, which he could see in the narrow slit between the curtain and the doorjamb, the man was still in the chair, tied and gagged. The two women were also in chairs, hands tied behind their backs, but their feet were not tied nor were they gagged. He cautiously moved closer to the doorway, looking for the others.

The two men came into the house from the porch and sat at the table. One at the chair at the end, the other, the smaller one called the Mex, sat on the bench, holding his knife before him, looking with squinted eyes from woman to woman and feeling the sharpness of the blade as he laughed softly. The women's eyes were wide and showed fear as they looked from one to the other and back at the knife-holding man. It was obvious what he had in mind for the three, but the other man, one Eli had not seen but at a distance, talked to the Mex. "You can have 'em after I'm done. I want that'n," nodding to the light-haired younger woman, "first." He laughed as he saw the fear in her eyes, looked back at his partner and laughed again.

"I thot ze boss said not to mess wit' ze wimmen?"

"Who's to know? He wants you to slit their throat, but he don't want us to mess with 'em? I ain't gonna tell him, are you?"

The Mex cackled, "Mebbe I take ze other one!" He

laughed as he drove the blade of the knife into the table-top, startling everyone, even his partner, the man known as Grant Lewis.

But Eli was surprised to hear a woman's voice, "But Grant, you promised…" pleaded the younger woman.

The other woman turned frowning as she looked at her sister, "Alma! What do you mean? Surely you didn't…"

The younger woman laughed, "What did you expect? There hasn't been another man around this place for months. What was I supposed to do? Become a nun or something? I don't want to end up as an old maid!" She turned her attention to the man she had called Grant, "Remember? You promised you would take care of me! After all I've done for you!" she smiled coyly, "And there's more," she promised.

"Alma! They're going to kill us! Don't you know that?" pleaded the dark-haired woman.

"All the more reason for me to save myself! Right Grant? You'll take me with you, won't you?"

"Honey, we've had our fun, but the boss don't allow no women. That's why we had to sneak around like we done," chuckled Grant, glancing from the girl to the Mex, grinning. "Love 'em an' leave 'em, that's what I always say."

"But, baby, you promised," pleaded the younger woman.

Both men laughed as Grant said, "We'll see, we'll see. Maybe if you treat me right, I'll keep you around a while."

"What about me, my frien'?" asked a cackling Mex.

"After I'm done. Be patient," he winked at the girl as if promising more.

CHAPTER 14

CONSEQUENCE

Eli thought of the other men, knowing the boss had instructed the two to be quiet about what was done, not that there was anyone near enough to hear anything, but he hoped the others were far enough away so they could not hear any gunshots. He shook his head to himself thinking he was not anxious to try to take these two with a knife, he was much more confident with Mr. Colt.

The women sat on either side of the doorway, their backs to the curtained passageway. The two men were at the table, Grant seated at the end, facing the curtain and the darkened back room, the Mex to the side, the table between him and Eli. The farmer was off to the right, his back to the open window. He was gagged, bound tightly, and although he struggled with his bonds, he was helpless.

Grant grinned at the Mex, leaned back in the chair, and asked, "How did you hook up with Ludvik, you weren't in the war?"

Antonio grinned, "I saw heem when he and the

others were running away. They had been in the prison, and I had many horses. I was Mesteñeros, a vaquero that caught wild horses, broke them, and sold them to the armies. He wanted the horses, made many promises, and I was tired of the mountains, so…" he shrugged.

"So, you are from Mexico? Not Texas?"

"Si, Sonora, Mexico, it was the land of mi Madre, she was a Yaqui, captured by mi Padre when he was a soldado. He did not treat her well." He chuckled at the memory. "She had all she could take, and one night she hit him hard with a big rock, knocked him out. When he came to, he was bound with rawhide on a stool, and she stood grinning as she held this knife," he held out the dagger that was his constant play toy, "She told him what she was going to do and he wet himself, cried, and begged. Just like she would when he beat her. I saw him do that and she had me watch. She cut off his clothes, then his ears and his nose and his tongue. He fought the rawhide, but it was no use. She used this knife," he held it before him as he grinned and remembered, "and slowly, very slowly," he stood, walked to the light-haired girl, stood behind her and pulled her hair back as he slowly ran the tip of the dagger across her throat, leaving a thin line of blood, "began to skin him, thin strips, from here," he touched her shoulder, cut through the blouse, "to here," he touched her waist, causing her to catch her breath. "Mi Madre said that I was not a Mex, but a Yaqui!" he snarled as he said it, shaking his head. "I should skin Ludvik like mi Padre!"

Antonio moved away from Alma and closer to Gwinn, taunting her in a similar fashion, pulling her hair back, running the tip of the knife across her throat. He laughed, "That is what Ludvik told me to do to these!" motioning to the women and the man. He glared at

Grant, back to the women, "So it is not if you save any for me, but if I save any for you." As he spoke, he walked toward the farmer, but kept his eyes on Grant.

Grant had been leaning back in the chair, front legs off the floor, but he dropped the chair to the floor, stood, and with his hand on the butt of his pistol, he looked at Antonio, "So, you want us to call you a Yaqui, instead of Mex?"

"I am Antonio Jose Maria Porfirio Lázaro Rodriguez. Pick one!" he growled, glaring at Grant.

"Alright, Antonio. We will do this together," he started toward the girl who made the promises, keeping his hand on the butt of his pistol that rested in a holster on his hip.

Eli had watched and listened from the darkness of the room behind the tattered curtain, saw the one called Grant coming toward the girl, but knew the most dangerous one was the Mex. He leaned to either side, trying to place the Mex, saw him near the farmer, but also saw the other one gripping the pistol as he neared the girl.

Eli could wait no longer. He slipped the Colt from the holster, lifted and cocked it. The ratcheting sound was loud in the little room and the sound stopped the man. Grant grabbed at his pistol at his hip, but Eli let the hammer drop and the .44 caliber Colt blasted, bucked, and belched smoke and lead as the bullet tore through the curtain and into the chest of the startled man who still gripped his pistol, lifted it, fought to bring it level, and squeezed off a shot. The pistol bucked, but the bullet tore into the belly of the bound woman before him. Her body jerked, her legs stiffened and relaxed as her head dropped to her chest. The outlaw dropped as his knees buckled and he fell to the floor, his eyes wide as blood blossomed at his chest. He grabbed at his shirt, fear staring at the dark room and the smoldering curtain as he fell to his face.

The older sister screamed as she watched her sister's life slip away. "Nooo, Alma, nooo!" as she tried to twist around and see where the shot came from. Gwinn stared at the dark doorway, glanced to the Mex who stood, cocking his arm back with the knife held above his head and let the slender missile whistle toward the curtain. The Mex grabbed for his holstered pistol. A grunt came from the dark room, as Eli grabbed at his right shoulder, to see the curtain pegged with the stiletto against his shoulder. His fingers were numbed, and he dropped the pistol from his right hand, felt it fall as it clattered on the floor.

He looked up to see the Mex dragging his pistol from the holster. Eli stepped to the side as he used his left hand to pull the LeMat from his belt at his back, cocking the weapon as he brought it up. The Mex fired, the bullet chipping wood from the doorjamb, making Eli duck to the side. He dropped to one knee, brought the LeMat up and flipped the lever on the hammer, squeezing the trigger. The pistol bucked and the bigger center muzzle spat fire, smoke, and a load of buckshot. The lead balls ripped the tabletop and tore into the torso of the knife-wielding Mexican, ripping holes in his fancy jacket, neck, and face. It is a terrible thing that buckshot does to its target and the man was instantly bloodied, but still stood. His face and neck looked like ground meat, blood dribbling as he tottered. The ratcheting of a hammer cocking came from the darkness, and he tried to lift his pistol, but the tongue of flame from the dark room spat smoke and lead as a big .40 caliber slug tore through the stillness and buried itself in the man's neck, driving him against the wall, making him slide down into a bloody heap at the end of the table.

Startled stillness filled the room, broken only by the ragged breathing and sniffling of the woman. Eli slowly stepped through the doorway, the LeMat pistol hanging at his side as a little tendril of smoke came from the barrels of the weapon. The room smelled of gunpowder and blood until the woman leaned forward and vomited. The farmer was visibly shaken and struggled at his bonds as he stared at the figure that stood in the doorway.

Eli went to the farmer, pulled his Bowie from the sheath at his back and cut the man free. He pulled off his bonds, loosed the bonds at his ankles, and tore the gag from his mouth. The farmer looked up at Eli, "Mister, whoever you are, you are a godsend!"

Eli nodded, handed his knife to the man, and sat down at the end of the table, watching as the farmer freed his woman. He turned to Eli, "Let us get that knife out and fix you up, alright?"

"Yeah, sure."

"Who are you, and how did you come to be here and help us?" asked the man as he sat down on the bench, breathing deep to get his wind before turning his attention to the bodies.

"I'm Eli McCain. I knew about these men and had followed them. But enough about that, how 'bout you draggin' out those bodies, and let your woman tend to this?" he touched the handle of the dagger that was in his shoulder, at least half the blade was buried in the muscle. He glanced at the woman who sat, face in her hands, as she sobbed for her sister. She sat erect, wiped her face with her apron, then with a visible resolve, stood and went to the cabinets to get the bandages and more that would be necessary to tend to Eli's wound. He looked to the man as he struggled with the body of the sister, but he managed to wrap her in a blanket and carry her to the porch. He would tend to her body come daylight.

————

THE WOMAN, Gwinn, was skilled at tending to wounds, having worked in a hospital during the war, and in a short while, Eli sat at the table, enjoying a fresh, hot cup of coffee. She stood leaning against the counter, her arms folded as she looked at Eli and her husband, a somber expression on her face and eyes that had gone glassy. He knew she was reflecting on the way her sister had talked just before she took the bullet and to watch her own sister die as she sat helpless and frightened that she might be next.

Eli looked at the man, Milton Hathcock, and asked, "How long had they been here?"

"Less than a week. The wagons came rollin' up, outriders with 'em, and I had no idea what they was doin'. I figgered they might be lookin' for grain or such for their animals. You know, you just don't expect three wagons and that many men all bein' outlaws. But when the big 'un, they called him Ludvik, stepped down and walked up an' stood right in front o' me, dragged iron an' told me what they was gonna do, there weren't nuthin' I could do, muh rifle was in the house, all I had in muh hand was a milk pail. An' he said if'n we did what we was told, wu'nt nobody get hurt. Then he said, 'I know you got wimmen in the house, so if you wan'em to be alright, do as yore told.'" He dropped his head, grabbed his coffee, and looked back to Eli, "What else could I do?"

"As far as it went, you did right. I ran into 'em back on the trail a ways, an' when I saw the wagons goin' to the river, I followed. They finagled their way into gettin' the cargo like they were legitimate freighters, and later I found the real freighters—wagons burnt, muleskinners killed. I reckon they got the paperwork from them before they killed 'em. I followed 'em here, but for all I knew, you were part of their gang. I didn't know about your womenfolk then."

Hathcock sipped at his coffee, looked over the cup to Eli, "So, what happens now?"

"They're headed into Helena, made a deal with a friend of mine at his store. But the vigilantes will be waiting for them."

"I shore don't want'em coming back here."

Eli dropped his eyes, slowly shook his head, and looked up to Hathcock and his woman. "I don't think they will be leaving Helena, but you need to be careful and always have your rifle within reach, just to be safe." He looked to Gwinn, "Do you have a pistol or rifle?"

She nodded, but did not answer, a heavy sigh lifting her shoulders as she wiped more tears from her eyes.

Eli said, "I'm almighty sorry about your sister. I just couldn't wait any longer. I heard the big man tell the Mex to do 'his thing' to the three of you and it was evident what he meant. I had to act, but I couldn't control what happened. I'm sorry."

She nodded, looked away, and walked into the bedroom and closed the door. Eli looked at Hathcock and the man responded, "She'll be alright. I think she's as hurt about what she learned about her sister, there at the end, as she is about her death. Those are not the memories you want to keep after you lose a family member."

"No, it's not." Eli stood, looked at the farmer, "I'm

going to get my horse, and if it's alright with you, I'll sleep in the barn, but I'll be leaving early in the morning."

"You're more than welcome to stay as long as you want. If it wasn't for you, I think we'd all be dead, so we are very grateful."

CHAPTER 15

EMPORIUM

When the sun showed its face in the east, tall cottonwoods that sided the Big Muddy stretched long shadows across the trail. Hills with rocky outcroppings and scattered piñon appeared to stretch a little higher to catch the first rays of the morning that lay a pale pink diaphanous blanket on the land. The big claybank stallion lifted his head a little higher as he stretched out on the trail. Eli had taken to the road just after midnight, anxious to overtake the outlaws and join forces with the vigilantes to greet the wagons when they entered Helena.

Rusty was a crossbreed Morgan and Tennessee Walker, and his long-legged gait, like the Walker, was ground eating and the Morgan gave him extraordinary stamina. Eli reached down and stroked the neck of the big horse, "You're the best, Rusty, we're about halfway there so how 'bout we take a break, get you some graze and both of us some rest." He nudged the horse to the riverbank, found a clearing with grass and access to the water, and stepped down. With little rest the night before, the wound in his shoulder, and nothing to eat for most of a day, Eli was ready to put on some coffee and dig out some biscuits given to him by Gwinn, the woman at the farm.

————

DUSK WAS DROPPING its curtain when a very tired Rusty walked into the livery to join the dapple-grey pack-horse. Eli slid down, held on to the saddle to get his legs under him, stepped back to see the smithy shaking his head, "Looks like you been in the saddle a while," he rumbled with his deep voice.

Eli let a bit of a grin split his face, shook his head, "Soon's I get him stripped and rubbed down, I'm hittin' the sack. Prob'ly won't wake up till sometime tomorrow," he mumbled as he led Rusty to the stall beside the grey.

But it was by the grey light of early morning that Eli stomped his feet into his boots and pulled his braces over his shoulders, slipped on his vest and hung his holstered Colt on his hip, the LeMat in his belt and the Bowie at his back. He did not feel dressed until his weapons were in place. He grabbed his hat off the dresser and stepped through the door. He was headed for Martine's Emporium; he did not want to miss out on what would be happening sooner than later.

Most businesses that catered to the gold seeking crowd did not have regular business hours other than sunup to sundown, and Martine was no different. When Eli walked up to the door, he saw Martine unlocking the front door and turning the sign around that said, *Open for Business*. The merchant grinned when he saw Eli approaching, opened the door wide and greeted him with, "Eli! Good to see you made it back! When'd you get in?"

"Just after dark, rode through the night before and all day to make it. I think we can expect the goods sometime this morning," explained Eli as he followed Martine into the store.

"I think John will be here shortly. When we talked yesterday, he guessed the freight would be showing up sometime this morning," explained Martine, walking behind the counter.

Eli pulled up a stool in front of the counter, put an elbow on the countertop, and said, "Did he and the others make up any kind of plan, what they're going to do?"

"Well, sort of, I think he was hoping to talk to you before they did anything, you know, get a better idea of what they would be up against. But he did talk to the others and they're ready to help."

Eli stood and walked to the front of the store to take a look out the windows, surveying the street and where the wagons might stop. He turned to Martine, "Do you have a back door, you know, for loading and unloading freight like we expect?"

"Yes, right through here," explained Martine, pointing to the door to the back room.

The alleyway was ample sized for teams and wagons, but not side by side. Although there other buildings that backed up to the alley, the space behind the brick building of the bank and emporium was a little greater than others, with a bit more set back. There were few fences or outbuildings, other than the usual outhouses and miscellaneous items, mostly junk, that was stacked behind buildings or near the alleyway. Eli walked out the back door, walked around to get a better idea and survey of the area to consider possibilities for both the outlaws and any of the vigilantes.

Martine stayed in the doorway of the back door, standing on a bit of a stoop, watching Eli make his survey. He heard someone enter the store and turned back to tend to the customer, leaving Eli to his planning. As Eli stepped back in, he heard a familiar voice and quickly checked his pistol, removing the thong on the hammer and ensuring it was loose in the holster. He stepped through the doorway, glanced to Martine who stood behind the counter, and saw the familiar face of Jonesy standing on the far side beside the big man he had thought of as the bully boss.

The big man scowled at Eli, back to Martine and to his sidekick, Jonesy, then to Eli, "I know you! You was on the trail a few days back! What'chu doin' here?"

Jonesy spoke up, "He's the partner to this'n. They's in this together!" explained Jonesy.

The bully boss scowled as he looked from Eli to Martine, growled "You got our money?"

Martine glanced to Eli and back to the men in front of the counter, "Yeah, I've got it. But I need to see the cargo."

"Why? We got three wagons full, that's all you need to know," growled Ludvik, glancing from Martine to Eli and back.

Martine said, "I'm not paying two thousand dollars, sight unseen."

Ludvik chuckled, "No, you ain't. You're payin' three thousand dollars or you ain't gettin' nuthin! There's others that'll gladly pay that!"

Martine glanced to Eli, saw a slight nod, and back to Ludvik. "Alright, it goes against the grain, but we need the goods, so, we'll pay it, but only if we can see the goods first!"

"You just make sure you got the money when we get back!" growled the big man, his paws on the counter as he leaned forward, his face inches from Martine's.

Martine's eyes flared, showing fear, and he leaned back, "Uh, uh, yeah. But I'll need to get it from the bank next door. I don't keep that much cash here."

"You'll have time, the wagons aren't here yet," he glanced up at the big clock, "It'll be about an hour. We'll pull up out back to unload. You can look at the stuff, then I get the money, then we'll unload," growled Ludvik, looking around the store.

Martine slowly nodded, still leaning back as far as the shelves behind him would allow and watched the big man. Ludvik balled his fists, and with eyes squinted, one eyebrow raised, he growled and turned away and started for the door.

His partner followed close behind as Ludvik slammed open the door, pushed aside two men that were just outside the door, and stomped away to the tethered horses to leave town. The two men looked after the big man and his partner, turned back to the store, and stepped inside. Martine had just let out his breath and took a deep one as he looked from Eli to the newcomers. Recognizing John Beidler, or X, and the second man, he spoke to Eli, "Here's X and Anton Holder, they're with the Committee."

X stepped to the counter, glanced to Eli and back to Martine. "Was that them?"

Eli spoke up, "That was them. The big man, Ludvik Kowalski, and his second, Karl Fischer. They said they'd be back in about an hour with the wagons. Of course, he demanded more money, which we agreed to pay after we see the goods."

"Good, good." He paused, thoughtful as he turned to face Eli, "How many men?"

"Six that I know of, he had eight but the other two won't be joining them. They ran into a little lead impediment."

X frowned, looking at Eli, but the expression of both men told the story and X slowly nodded his head. "Any ideas?"

Eli stepped closer, motioned to Martine to hand him a piece of paper as he grabbed up a stub of a pencil. He began drawing a layout of the alley, the existing buildings he took note of when he made his survey and began to explain what he thought might be a good tactic. When he finished, X looked at Eli, "Was you in the army?"

"Lieutenant Colonel in Sherman's cavalry."

"Thought so. Looks good. The others are waitin' in the café 'cross the street. I'll lay this out fer 'em, and we'll be in place in just a short while. We'll wait for your sign or action, 'fore we move on 'em. But we'll be ready and the boys up top will have 'em all covered."

Eli nodded, shook hands with X, and watched as he and Anton left the store. He looked at Martine, "I like him. Acts like a man to ride the river with."

"I think so. His reputation is good, folks speak highly of him. He was a leader of the vigilantes in Virginia City before coming here." Martine turned to look at Eli, "I'm mighty thankful for your help in this, don't know how I'll ever repay you."

"No need, besides, it ain't over yet," chuckled Eli. He reached down for his Winchester that he had leaned against the back of the counter when he came in, did a quick check of the weapon, and started for the back.

Martine followed him and before opening the back door, Eli said, "Uh, 'fore they come, you might want to have a rifle or at least a pistol handy, but out of sight."

Martine chuckled, "I'm not a very good shot, haven't done much hunting or shooting, but," he grinned as he looked up at Eli, "I've got a Colt revolving shotgun that I'll have close by."

Eli chuckled, "That'll do it."

CHAPTER 16

ENSNARE

The bank building with the emporium was on the corner of Sixth Street and Last Chance Gulch. Sixth, running east and west, crossed the main street at the base of a slight rise in the main road. Eli stood out front, leaning on the hitchrail and watching for the wagons. It was the main street of the business area and at this time of day, there were many people on the boardwalk, the street, and in the many stores. Horses stood hipshot at the hitchrails, mostly in front of the many saloons, and farm or miners' wagons were standing in front of the different stores of interest to the miners. Two wagons were in front of Martine's Emporium, both with double hitches and partially loaded with the miner's weekly supplies of food, grain for the animals, and additional miner's supplies.

A bit of a ruckus caught his attention as the three wagons, each with a four-up of mules, clattered over the slight rise and started toward the store. The wagons passed the corner, swung wide and started up the alleyway behind the building, directed by the big boss who was riding an equally big bay horse that he manhandled with rough ways. Eli shook his head knowing that anyone that mistreated his horse was not a man to be trusted, but he expected little else from a man that had little or no regard for the value of human life, willing to have a family murdered for his own benefit of a few dollars.

Eli watched as the man directed the wagons into the alleyway, gave a gruff nod to Eli, and followed the wagons. Eli turned back into the store, nodding to Martine who was waiting on some customers. Martine spoke to Amélie and followed Eli into the back room.

The double doors opened wide, and Eli had his rifle just behind the open door, as did Martine with his shotgun. They stood on the bit of a stoop, watching as the wagons pulled closer, the one in the lead stopping with the tailgate near the back door. On the far side of the wagons, Ludvik stepped down from his mount, tied the horse off to the wagon, and walked around the back to face Martine and Eli. He dropped the big tailgate, motioned to the stacked goods, and nodded for the two to come take their look.

Eli deferred to Martine, letting him nose around the boxes, barrels, and crates, noting the markings on the crates and barrels. He climbed up on the wagon, looking at the sacks of grain, barrels of flour and cornmeal. He looked down at Ludvik, "This looks good, and if the other wagons are the same, we've got a deal." He climbed over the containers to drop off the side of the wagon and started to the other wagons. Ludvik stopped him, "You've seen 'nuff. Get muh money, now!" he barked, standing close to Martine and pushing up against him. He glared at Eli as he started to come near, barked to the driver of the wagon, "Keep a watch on this'n Karl. Me'n him," nodding to Martine, "will get the money!"

Karl stood with one knee on the seat, the other foot in the box, as he looked over the cargo in the wagon and lifted his rifle as he grinned at Eli who stepped back, hands out to the side. Eli glanced to Martine, nodded, and turned to the side, his left side with his Colt away from Karl. He glanced to the rooftops, and to the end of the alley, just as Martine stepped inside the back door. Eli slipped the Colt from the holster, dropped to one knee, and brought the pistol to bear on Karl and fired. The .44 caliber Colt Army bucked and belched lead and smoke, the bullet taking Karl in the base of his throat. Karl's eyes flared as he was driven back by the force of the slug, blood blossomed on his throat as he struggled to take a breath, lift his rifle, or squeeze off a shot, but he was already dead even though he did not know it. His body crumpled into the wagon box, disappearing from sight.

The blast of the shot from Eli signaled the vigilantes to open fire and the sudden thunder of gunfire rattled the windows and startled the mules. The two men that had been outriders with Ludvik kicked out of their saddles and dropped behind the wagons, but they were not protected as the shooters had taken up positions on both sides and ends of the alley, blocking them all in place.

Shouts, curses, screams, and gunfire and gunsmoke filled the narrow alleyway between the two rows of back-to-back businesses. After the first volley, Eli had stepped into the back door, expecting to see Ludvik and Martine, but the back room was empty. In the pause between volleys, Eli shouted, "You men with the wagons, you have no way out. Throw down your weapons and stand with your hands up!" There were moans coming from wounded men, reminding Eli of the many battles in the war when the wounded were left on the field of battle and continued to cry for help but receiving none. He hollered again, "Give it up or die!"

He spotted one man crawling, dragging a bloody leg, from behind the wagon and toward the mules. He had a pistol in hand and Eli did not think he was giving up and followed him with the sights of the Winchester. The man was between the teams of mules, belly down, lifted on one elbow and started to bring up his pistol, but a nervous mule let loose with a kick that caught him on his jaw, knocking him into the mule behind, who reached down and bit a chunk of flesh out of his arm. The man struggled to get away, but another kick from the recalcitrant mule sent him rolling across the dirt and into the fence post on the far side. Eli chuckled, shook his head, and started to call out again, but gunfire erupted again until the shooters of the vigilantes realized there was no return fire. They stopped and Eli stepped out of the door and started toward the wagons, pistol at the ready as he went from man to man, kicking away weapons or tossing them aside. Of the five outlaws, three were so badly riddled with bullets there was no life left in them, two had at least two, if not more, wounds and lay against the wagon wheels, blood seeping from their wounds.

Anton Holder stepped from the door to the store-room, looked for Eli and spotting him motioned him to come near. As he approached, "That big man—Ludvik, I think you said his name was—has Martine's woman and is demanding the money and a way out. He didn't see me; he was just talking to Martine when the other people in the store ran out."

"Where is he?"

"At the counter, by the register. He has a gun to her head an' says he'll kill her."

"What'd Martine do?"

"He said the money was upstairs in their home and Ludvik sent him after it."

Eli quickly pictured the store and the stairs to the living quarters, the layout of the counters, tables, and such, and with a nod to Anton, "You keep this," handing him the Winchester, "and stay near the door. I've got my pistol and he'll prob'ly want me to put it down, which I will. But if you get a clear shot, you take it, otherwise just let me handle it."

Anton nodded, accepted the rifle and opened the breech to be sure there was a cartridge in the chamber, closed the breech with the lever, and followed Eli to the door. Eli slowly opened the door, heard Ludvik, "If you're the partner, come on out, NOW!" he demanded. Eli started through the door, hands held high as he looked at the big man holding Amélie in front of him, his big arm around her neck and a pistol to the side of her head. He growled, "Put your shooter on the table there, and move away!"

"Alright, alright, just take it easy. Where's Martine?"

"He's gettin' the money. Said it was upstairs." He glanced to the stairs, pointed the pistol to the ceiling and fired a shot and hollered, "Hurry up, or I'm gonna kill her!"

"Easy, easy. No reason to get upset. He'll be down. He said he had it in a strongbox and might have to find the key. You probably have him so scared he can't find nothing!" stated Eli, slowly lowering his hands as he talked. He was standing between two counters that were stacked with items of clothing on display, with cabinets below. He knew he could drop and be out of the line of fire, but that would put Amélie in more danger and the big man was out of patience, if he ever had any in the first place.

Eli spoke again, looking up at the ceiling, "I hear him movin' around up there, he's prob'ly gettin' in the strongbox and will come right down."

Ludvik just growled, pulled the woman even closer making her grab at his arm so she could breathe, but she could not move. Her eyes were filled with fear as she looked around the store, but there was no hope for her in anything she saw until she looked at Eli who had turned away slightly and winked so only she could see, and she opened wide her eyes in either hope or fear, but Eli took it for hope.

The door to the rooms upstairs pushed open and they could see the feet of Martine as they touched the first stairs. Eli watched Ludvik who had turned to see the man on the stairs, Eli signaled Amélie to bite the man's arm and drop. She blinked her eyes to say she understood but Ludvik pulled her tight again as he turned back to watch Eli. But Martine, seeing Eli, glanced to the side to see his wife and the big man, back to Eli and stumbled on the stairs and slammed against the rail, grunted, and stumbled again. It was enough to get Ludvik's attention which gave a little slack to his grip and Amélie sunk her teeth in his arm. He jerked his arm away, enabling her to drop to the floor.

At the first move of Martine, Eli slipped his hand behind his back and gripped the LeMat, dragged it out of his belt and brought it level with the big man's chest and Eli pulled the trigger. Before the smoke cleared from the first shot, he quickly flipped the lever on the hammer and cocked it again, firing the shotgun slug of buckshot at the big man. The first bullet blossomed red on his chest, making him turn his pistol toward Eli, but the blast from the buckshot load peppered his face, neck, and chest, driving him back against the shelves. The weight of the big man made the shelves crumple, dropping cans of fruit and more on his head as he slid to the floor, all the shelves cascading on top of him as he tried to suck wind, but got only blood. He struggled to get out from under the shelves, but Eli had stepped closer, Amélie had run away, and Martine ran to his woman. Eli saw the big man pushing aside broken shelves as he spat blood and curses. When his face showed, he was staring at the muzzle of Eli's pistol as Eli leaned over the counter on his elbows and watched the beast fight his way free of the rubble.

When he was free of the entanglements but still on the floor, he looked at Eli through the blood on his head and face, glared hatred and wiped blood away as he growled. "I'm gonna kill you!"

Eli grinned, "How, you're already dead?!" Eli looked to the doorway to the back room where Anton stood, Winchester in hand, waiting. With a nod of his head, Eli motioned the man forward, "I'll help you get him up and outside to the others. This'n is the boss of the bunch." Anton nodded, sat the Winchester aside and the two men struggled with the bloody big man, but soon had him between them and carried him to the back door where another of the vigilantes took Eli's place. X came near, "He the one called Ludvik?"

"That's him," answered Eli, watching the others drop the big man to the ground beside the two other wounded men. "They all that's left?" asked Eli, nodding toward the pair, recognizing the one as the casualty of the mule kick.

"Yup. The other three were shot to doll rags, served

'em right." X motioned for Anton to come close as he turned to Eli, "So, tell me 'bout 'em."

Eli started with, "I first saw them with a pair of wagons headin' toward Helena on the Mullan Road, then when I saw their tracks cuttin' toward the river, it got my curiosity up so I followed..." he continued to tell about the loading of the cargo from the riverboat using the stolen Bill of Lading, about the other burnt wagons and murdered muleskinners, the farm and the people, and the attempted extortion of Martine. "That's about it."

"You heard him tell his men to murder the farm family?"

"That's right, and I heard it again from the two men when they started to do the deed."

"You stopped 'em?" asked X.

Eli nodded, dropping his eyes to the ground at the memory of the fight, "That's when the one known as Grant shot the girl, but I think he was trying to get me."

X looked at Anton, nodded, and with a nod to Eli, X led the others to take the wounded men away. He called back over his shoulder, "We'll take care of the bodies, you and Martine can do what you will with the mules and wagons."

CHAPTER 17

REUNION

The sounds of footsteps came from upstairs and with a quick look around, Eli saw the sign on the door had been turned to *Closed*. He started up the stairs, rapped on the door, and was greeted by a visibly shaken Martine. "Eli! Come in, come in." As he stepped in, Eli saw Amélie sitting on the divan and reaching for a cup that sat near a teapot.

Martine said, "Please, join us. We're just having a bit of tea and you are welcome." He motioned to a wingback chair, "Would you like some tea, or would you prefer coffee?"

Eli grinned as he seated himself, "I've never been much of a tea drinker, but you don't have to fix coffee just for me."

"Nonsense. Nothing is too good for you, you saved us from..." he shook his head and turned to the corner nook of a kitchen, letting the thoughts hang in the air.

Amélie forced a smile, but she was obviously still traumatized, the teacup shaking in her hand as she lifted it to her lips. She sat the cup back on the saucer, sat them on the table, and looked at Eli. "Have you seen the Hamiltons or the Williamses since you've been in town?" She was clearly wanting to have the topic of discussion to be something more pleasant than the recent happenings.

"No, but I was planning on finding them, see how they're doing."

"Harriet Hamilton and the children have settled in their new home. It's a lovely place just up from the corner of State Street and Davis. Harriet said the Williamses were looking for farmland, but with all the gold claims and such, well…" she shrugged, reaching for her teacup again.

"I'm glad to hear the Hamiltons are settled. They were a little concerned since they hadn't heard much from her husband, Cyrus."

"With three months on board that riverboat, *Louella*, we had plenty of time to get acquainted, and we became friends with both the Hamiltons and the Williamses. Both ladies were fine women and the children also."

Eli was not one to carry on with conversations in the way of women and was relieved when Martine brought him a steaming cup of coffee. He gladly accepted it, lifted it to his mouth, and savored the interruption and the flavor of the strong black brew. Martine was seated beside his wife and sat his coffee on the table before them. He looked at Eli, "We also saw and talked with another man you might remember, Chaplain Haney?"

"Yes, I've known the chaplain since the war. So, he's here in Helena?"

"He is, and he's holding services tomorrow with the Reverend E.T. McLaughlin of the St. Paul's Methodist Episcopal Church down on Joliet Street. If you'd like to come with us, I'm sure we'll see the Hamiltons and maybe the Williamses. It would be good to have a reunion with those that went through so much with us on the trip up the Missouri, don't you think so, Eli?"

Eli grinned, let a bit of a snicker escape as he smiled up at the couple, "You know, I think that'd be just fine. I'd like to see the others, maybe talk to a few folks that have been around the area for a while, see if I can find out some news about my boys. Yeah, that'll be just fine." He lifted the coffee cup for another long sip of the steaming java.

————

SUNDAY DID NOT SHOW itself as being much different from a weekday, the streets were still busy, many of the stores were open, saloons were just as boisterous, and prospectors had their noses in the sluices and rocker boxes. Eli walked with Martine and Amélie from their store heading south on Main Street or as many still called it, Last Chance Gulch. As they walked, Martine talked about the church. "Although we've only been one time, the preacher does a fine job, and the people are friendly. It's growing, just like the rest of the town, and the little building just won't hold very many. I'm certain they will be building something bigger right soon."

As they neared the small clapboard-covered log building, several people were standing on the boardwalk, visiting, while others were carrying the benches from inside to line them up outside on the empty lot just south of the building. It was evident the crowd would be too big for the little building and the services would be held outside. Eli looked up at the clear blue sky, felt the warmth of the morning sun, and smiled, knowing it would be a good day for the services.

Eli spotted Chaplain Haney, waved, and walked to him. "Can I be of help, Chaplain?"

"Eli, it is good to see you, my friend." He looked at the others that were carrying out the benches and more and back to Eli, "I think these men have things well in hand." He turned his attention back to Eli, "So, still looking for your twins?"

"I am, chaplain, I am. No word since I heard they had gone to the goldfields, and I'll start looking around for them first thing tomorrow. I've been with the Beaumonts the last couple days, but I'll start my search tomorrow."

"Well, I've been praying for you and your sons, I'm certain you'll find them soon. Now, if you'll excuse me?"

Eli nodded as the chaplain joined the young man who was the pastor of the church, the Reverend E.T. McLaughlin, who stepped behind the pulpit and lifted his hands, "Folks, welcome to the St. Paul's Methodist Episcopal Church. We have such a big crowd this morning, we had to move our services outdoors. Please allow the ladies to be seated first. Gentlemen, if you'll stand to the side or be seated on the grass or the few blankets we have, we'll get started."

In short order everyone was seated, some couples choosing to sit together on the blankets, several men stood around the edges, and the crowd numbered close to a hundred. Pastor McLaughlin lifted his hands again, and said, "Join me as we sing, 'He Leadeth Me.'"

Everyone stood and began to sing with the pastor.

He leadeth me, O blessed thought!
O words with heav'nly comfort fraught!
Whate'er I do, where'er I be
Still 'tis God's hand that leadeth me.
He leadeth me, He leadeth me,

By His own hand He leadeth me;
His faithful foll'wer I would be,
For by His hand He leadeth me.

The congregation enjoyed singing and the pastor led them in another old hymn, "The Strife is O'er, the Battle Done." At its conclusion, the pastor introduced Chaplain Haney and stepped back for the man to assume the pulpit.

Chaplain Haney began, "Thank you so much for the opportunity, Pastor." He looked at the congregation who was now seated and the many standing, "I'd like to take my message this morning from the Gospel of Mark, chapter eight, beginning with verse thirty-four. *And when he had called the people unto him with his disciples also, he said unto them, Whosoever will come after me, let him deny himself, and take up his cross and follow me. For whosoever will save his life shall lose it; but whosoever shall lose his life for my sake and the gospel's the same shall save it. For what shall it profit a man, if he shall gain the whole world, and lose his own soul? Or what shall a man give in exchange for his soul?* I would like to focus our attention on verse thirty-six and thirty-seven. God asks us, what do we get if we gain the whole world and lose our soul? And I'd like to ask you that same thing this morning.

"We are in a time and place where it seems everything is focused on getting gold. Men have left families behind and sacrificed everything in hopes of finding riches in the Rockies. True, some have found gold, a few have even become rich in the doing of it, but so many more have sacrificed everything and gained nothing but blisters, bunions, and bad manners.

"But what if? What if you find gold, and lots of it, but lose your soul in the doing? We might think it a good exchange, at least while we live and enjoy the riches, but the Bible tells us we have a life-span of threescore and ten, that's seventy years, if we're lucky. How many of us know others that have left this world many years short of seventy? Umhmm, most of us.

"My friends, life is short, and eternity is long. If we gain the riches of gold but do not prepare for eternity to the saving of our soul, it will all be for naught. The Bible tells us many things about those that do not make those preparations, it tells us that the destiny of those without Christ is Hell forever! Did you know that in Hell you will have all your five senses? You will smell nothing but burning sulphur or brimstone, see nothing but darkness, hear nothing but the agonizing screams of others, taste nothing but thirst and sulphur, feel nothing but ever-lasting pain! Is that what you want? What good will a pocket of gold nuggets do you then?

"*Behold, now is the accepted time, behold, now is the day of salvation.* Those are words from the book of Corinthians, chapter six and verse two. Those words apply to you today. Would you rather gain the whole world and lose your soul? If not, do something about it today."

The chaplain began the invitation by telling everyone about what they must do, "First, you must understand that you are a sinner, Romans 3:23, and because we're sinners, there is a penalty and that penalty is death and hell forever, Romans 6:23. But, and this is the best part, *God showed his love toward us in that while we were yet sinners Christ died for us.* Romans 5:8. When He died, He purchased the gift of eternal life for us, Romans 6:23, and it's a gift that you must receive to save your soul, Romans 10:9-10, 13. Wouldn't you like to do that today? If you do, then while our heads are bowed and others pray, won't you come forward and let Pastor McLaughlin pray with you?"

Several of the men that were standing around the outside of the crowd, began walking to the front, heads bowed, some with tears streaming down their faces. Two couples stood and went forward also, among them Martine and Amélie Beaumont. Eli watched as many knelt at the front, listening to the pastor explain the plan to them, and together, many prayed to accept the free gift of salvation purchased by Christ on the cross. When the prayer ended and everyone stood, the others applauded and muttered many amens as the crowd rejoiced together.

After the service, Eli met with the Hamiltons and Harriet introduced him to her husband, Cyrus, who shook hands and said, "I want to thank you for watching out for my family. You were a definite answer to prayer. I had worried about them every day until they arrived and that was a blessed day."

"I enjoyed spending time with your family. You are a very blessed man!" declared Eli, grinning at Ben and Maribel, the daughter of the Williamses. "Of course, keeping track of Ben was almost a full-time job!" he kidded as he grinned at the young couple.

It was a good time of reunion of the families that had befriended one another on the trip up the Missouri aboard the *Louella* riverboat. They had spent three months of some of the most challenging days in their lives together and had weathered attacks by Sioux, gunrunners, and some bad weather. But they prevailed and their friendships were cemented in the travails. The families reminisced, shared their time at the pot-luck lunch that was the usual pattern of the church, and talked with some of the other members.

As they shared their plans and committed to getting together as often as possible in the coming days, they readied to part with handshakes, hugs, and promises, and went their separate ways.

When Eli returned to the Paynes hotel, he took time to check on his horses and gear, fed the animals a bit of grain, gave them a good brushing, and promised, "Now, in the morning, we're gonna start our search. It might take a while, but we've got a lot of ground to cover, so don't go gettin' lazy on me, y'hear?" He was certain Rusty understood as he turned to look at him, then shook his head up and down, but maybe he was just asking for more grain.

CHAPTER 18

SEARCH

There was very little to distinguish the twins from one another. While their appearances differed little, it was their demeanor or personality that allowed others to tell them apart. Although in their growing-up years, Joshua usually took the lead and was the more dominant of the two, the roles gradually reversed as the boys grew to manhood. Now it was Jubal that had become the more outgoing, often showing a broad smile and a ready greeting, impulsive in his decisions and commitments. Joshua had matured in a way that caused him to be become the thoughtful one, choosing to consider the problem before making his choice, but once made, he often acted quickly and even somewhat impulsively. Maybe it was mistakes made and learned from, such as their desertion from the Union Army, but kindness and thoughtfulness had become his mantra.

The two young men lay in their blankets under the pine bough lean-to, doing what had become their long-held habit, discussing the day's events and preparing for the morrow. Jubal had been sharing his ideas and plans for their future, "And if we work hard, we should get a nice nest egg in, oh, maybe a couple months. Then we can start lookin' for our own claim. Now that we've learned about sluicing and such, we could do quite well."

Joshua mumbled a "Ummhmm" as he reached down to his side and brought up a closed fist to show Jubal. As he opened his hand to show his brother two thumbnail-sized nuggets, he watched Jubal's reaction.

"When did you get these?" he asked as he turned them over and over to look at every detail. He hefted them in his hand, judging the weight of each one.

"Today, when we were digging in the hillside. You saw that vein same as I did, and, well, when I saw these, I couldn't resist."

"But that's stealin'! Ain't that what they call high-grading?"

"Ummhmm. But remember when we were buildin' that sluice, the Long Tom, for them and they promised that the more they get, the more we get?"

"Yeah, I remember," responded Jubal, still looking at the nuggets.

"And we haven't seen any more, at least not like them. They've more than doubled their take, all cuz o' what we built, and they haven't increased our poke any. I reckon that," nodding to the nuggets, "is just what we deserve, an' maybe that ain't enough."

"I dunno, brother, if they knew what'chu done, no tellin' what they'd do. I heard the other day about some claim owner takin' things to the miner's court and his hired hand had to give up all his takin's an' they run him outta the territory! Some said he was lucky they didn't hang him!"

"We ain't gonna get hung. I figger if we can get a little

more, maybe in the next couple days, they won't even know we got it, and we can hightail it outta here with our pockets full."

Jubal, the more impulsive of the two was a little reticent, but the two nuggets weighed heavy in his hand and on his mind. "It would sure make it easier for us to leave and sooner too! We'd have time to stake a claim and do some good panning or sluicing 'fore winter comes. Maybe even get enough to where we could be long gone 'fore snow flies!" He chuckled as he begrudgingly handed the nuggets back to his brother. He took a deep breath and shook his head, "Dunno if I'm gonna get any sleep tonight!"

Jubal rolled over, his back to his brother, as his mind raced with possibilities. He frowned, rolled to his back, "Where d'ya think we oughta go? You know, to find us a claim?"

Joshua chuckled, "When those two came through yes'tiddy, the big 'un was talkin' to Levi and Evan, and I talked to the other'n. He said they heard about some good claims up Confederate Gulch, a place they're callin' Diamond City."

"Where's that?"

"Th'other side of the river, into the Big Belt Mountains o'er yonder. He said he heard they was gettin' shovels full o' dust an' nuggets. Beats everthin' he ever heard before. I figger the sooner we can get there, the better claim we can get, the more gold we can get," explained Joshua.

———

THE STILLNESS of the early morning was Eli's favorite time of day, especially when he was sitting his saddle aboard the big red dun stallion who answered to Rusty. The thin grey line at the eastern horizon was beginning to blush pink as he took to the trail that followed a dry creek bed that held water only during the spring runoff, or times of heavy rain. Rusty tossed his head and side-stepped as he looked to the bottom of the draw toward a scraggly ponderosa. Eli pulled the stallion to a stop, squinted as he looked at the shadowy skeletal tree. Two bodies hung from the big branch that stretched toward the town. With the slow-rising sun in his face, Eli could not make out the figures and nudged Rusty a bit closer. As he neared, Rusty grew skittish, tossing his head and sidestepping, but Eli was close enough to recognize the two men as the big boss of the freighter gang, Ludvik Kowalski, and another of the gang that had been kicked aside by the mule. Scribbled signs hung on their chests to identify them only as murderers and thieves hung by the Committee of Safety. Eli slowly shook his head, reined Rusty back to the trail and pushed on, the image of the two men branded in his memory.

As they rode into the sunrise, he turned his attention to the memory of conversations of yesterday when he had talked with Pastor McLaughlin and a couple of the men who had been among the early gold seekers. Although none knew of twins that were looking for work in the goldfield, they did give him some places to start his search. The pastor shared, "I've heard some talking about Montana City and the upper reaches of Prickly Pear Creek, others have talked about Ten Mile Creek, and of course your friend, Cyrus, has his claim at the conflu-ence of Ten Mile and Blue Cloud."

The other man, Bradford Lewis, added, "As you've prob'ly heard, gold is where you find it, and one place is as good as another. I've heard talk of Elkhorn, Marysville, a new one called Diamond City, and just about any place that's near running water, you'll find somebody pannin' the gravel."

Eli shook his head at the memory knowing what had been said did little to narrow his search, although none had heard anything of twins on the hunt for work. But he thought that alone was a good thing, for if they had been in trouble, they would be known. Although his search had not been narrowed, he knew he had a lot of ground to cover.

Helena was fading behind him when he neared a point of a long ridge that was thick with black timber on the north-facing slope. As he topped the long bench, another small ridge, much like the first, rose from a dry wash and nudged the trail around its north face. While the north-facing slopes of the hills were black with thick timber, the south slopes were freckled with a few fir and spruce but were mostly bald and held only grassy slopes. While the flats held lush meadows and parks, separated by tall ponderosa, fir, and spruce. It was beautiful country that had been marred by the prospect holes of gold seekers.

The rolling hills offered a variety of sights and views, while the mist of early morning lay in the low valleys. The haze from the cool of the night, hung like a thin curtain masking the furthermost hills that rose like rows upon rows of ever diminishing insurmountable mounds. The trail dropped him into the mouth of a long draw that showed an unorganized collection of sun faded clap-board-sided buildings that made up the infant town of Montana City. He pushed on through the outskirts of the little settlement, unheard and unseen by anyone except one lazy hound dog that lifted his head and let out a mournful howl and dropped his sorrowful face between his paws and paid little more attention to the passerby.

The sun was full up, but the Prickly Pear Creek chuckled its way between the hills that showed heavy black timber and long shadows that lay across the valley bottom. Eli reined up at a break in the willows that showed a gravelly bottom crossing. He stepped down and allowed the horses to drink while he scanned the hillsides and the shadowy valley before them. The crossing was less than fifty yards from a pair of wall tents that sat on the east bank of the creek, just above the rough road that showed recent passage of wagons. As he stood beside Rusty, he saw the tent flap of one of the wall tents flip aside and a whiskery-faced man with a potbelly covered only by the faded red union suit stepped out, stretched and yawned as he pulled the braces over his shoulders and started to the trees.

Eli grinned as he swung back aboard the claybank stallion and pushed across the creek that was no more that fifteen feet across and about eighteen inches deep at best. The horses splashed across the water and took to the wagon road as they turned south to face upstream of the draw. When he neared the first camp, he reined up and called out, "Hello, the camp! I'm friendly, can I come in?"

The man that had gone to the trees quickly showed himself, "Who're you an' what'chu want?"

Eli saw the man had a pistol stuck in the front of his britches and his hand rested on the butt. Eli nodded, "Mornin'! Just want to ask you a question. I'm lookin' for a couple fellas, thought you might have seen 'em."

"You the law?" he asked, frowning at Eli and looking over the horses and gear.

"No, I'm not the law, but I am looking for couple

fellas, twins. Both have dark hair, average height and build, good-lookin' fellas."

"What'chu want 'em fer?" asked the prospector, motioning for Eli to step down.

As Eli swung down, he stood beside Rusty and answered, "They're my sons. Their ma sent me after 'em, wants 'em to come home."

The man slowly lifted his head, cocking one eyebrow high as he took the measure of the man before him. "I'm 'bout to fix some coffee, light a spell and we'll talk."

Eli nodded, grinning, and dropped the lead of Rusty. Ground tied, he knew the horses would not drift too far, but would take as much graze as they wanted. He loosened the girths on both Rusty and the grey, then walked to the fire, seated himself on a stub of a stump, and watched the coffeepot do its dance on the rock.

"I'm Red, Red O'Brien. Muh partner's Blake, only name he goes by." Red reached for the cups, poured two full and handed a steaming cup to Eli. "I saw couple fellas that might be who you're lookin' fer. They was workin' fer a claim upstream, Mallory an' Donahue's claim. The two was doin' most o' the work while the partners kept pannin'. They built a Long-Tom fer 'em. But last I heard, they cut out for the tall an' uncut!"

Eli dug in his pocket for the tintype, handed it to Red, and asked, "That them?"

Red frowned, held the tintype at arm's length, moved it back and forth to catch the sunlight, and answered, "Think so. After all, don't see twins very often."

"How long ago did they leave?"

"Dunno fer shore. I'm thinkin' it was sometime last week. Ol' Donahue come down'chere, madder'n an ol' wet hen, lookin' fer 'em. Said they up and took off without so much as a by yore leave. He thought they mighta been high-gradin' but he weren't sure, that's somethin' that's hard to prove," chuckled Red, sipping his coffee. As he finished his spiel, he looked up to see his partner, Blake, coming from his wall tent, frowning and fussing as he ran his fingers through his hair and whiskers. He found something, popped it between his thumbnail and fingernail, and growled at his partner, "Why'nt'cha wake me?"

"Why? You ain't worth a plug till you have yore coffee an' you're plumb cantankerous even then. I was enjoyin' a peaceful visit with our new friend instead o' puttin' up wit' yore abuse!" grumbled Red, chuckling as he spoke, the movement making his belly bounce as he talked.

Blake grumbled as he picked up a cup and poured himself some coffee. He glanced to Eli, sat down and grumbled some more as he sipped at the coffee and scratched his belly, side, and back, looking for the many bugs he was known to carry. Red looked at his partner, "Eli here is lookin' for his boys, twins, that come out to the goldfields. I tol' him the only ones we knowed was them that worked fer Donahue an' Mallory."

Blake grunted, squinted at Eli, and took another sip of coffee. Eli shook his head, finished his coffee, threw out the dregs, and handed the cup back to Red. "Thanks for the coffee. I think I'll ride on and go talk to those two, see if they have any idea where the boys went."

"You be careful. Those two can be dangerous, they'd just as soon shoot as not. There's been some fellas trying to jump some claims an' they ain't takin' no chances. Watch yourself!"

"I will, and thanks again," replied Eli as he tightened the girths and swung aboard Rusty, reined around and started upstream, hopeful of learning more about his boys.

CHAPTER 19

NEWS

T he bullet whiffed by his ear at the same time he heard the gunshot. In an instant, he grabbed the stock of the Winchester, kicked his foot free of the right stirrup and bailed off the left side of the big stallion. He slapped Rusty on the rump and dove behind a rock and cluster of oak brush. Another bullet ricocheted off the rock, knocking a chip against his arm as he lifted the Winchester Yellowboy and jacked a round in the chamber. He saw the puff of smoke just past the bottom of the long sluice box and picked his target just under the long-tom. He squeezed off a round, heard the yelp of a man hit, and jacked another round as he rolled to the other side of the boulder.

Eli searched for a target, saw the top of a hat moving along the sluice and put a bullet into it, sending it flying as the hatless and bald head dove under cover of the rockpile. He guessed there were at least two shooters, maybe more. He carefully parted the brush with the barrel of his rifle, looking at the camp that had been described to him as the one where the twins had been working. A bullet smashed through the brush and splattered against the rock, followed by a flurry of shots that came rapidly and ripped through the brush, some whining off the boulder, others whistling through the brush and past Eli.

He rolled back to the low side of the boulder, bellied down and tried to look under the brush, but the clatter of hooves and a shout showed two riders, laying low on the necks of the horses and slapping their mounts with the barrels of their rifles as they took off down the road just traveled by Eli. One man had a mop of red hair that showed under his floppy felt hat, broad shoulders and riding a big bay. The other was bald, with a friar ring of hair just over his ears. He was a smaller man, blood showing on his right leg, and he was riding a black with two stockings. Eli jumped to his feet, started to shoot but knew it was a waste of bullets. He looked to the camp, saw no movement, and carefully started across the little creek. He whistled the usual three tone call to his horses and by the time he climbed the far bank, both horses were splashing across the water behind him.

With his rifle at his hip, Eli walked through the camp. At the low end of the long-tom sluice, a bloody body lay contorted as overflow spilled out around him. Eli looked around, back at the dead man, and pulled him away from the spillage. He walked toward the two wall tents, saw a boot sticking out from one, and cautiously walked closer. He pushed aside the flap with the muzzle of the rifle, saw a man lying on his side, blood on a leg and shoulder. Eli nudged the boot with his foot, saw a little movement and heard a low groan. With a quick look around the camp, Eli returned to the man's side and rolled him to his back. His eyes fluttered open, and with a frown wrinkling his face, he squinted at Eli, "Who're you?"

"I'm a friend. What happened here?"

"Poke robbers…they was after…our dust." He struggled to talk, moaned from the pain of the two wounds, and faded in and out of consciousness. Eli pushed aside the cot, stretched out the blanket on the ground, and rolled the man onto it to work on his wounds. He looked around for anything to use as bandages, or something medicinal for the wounds. After fetching a pail of water and some rags from the other tent, Eli returned and began cleaning the wounds. He had gathered a few pads of prickly pear and once the wounds were clean, he peeled the pads to use the gelatinous centers to cover the wounds. Once that was done, he bound up the wounds as tightly as he could and lifted the man's head to put it on a folded blanket.

He sat back on his heels, watched the man's eyelids flutter, and a moan escape his lips. When his eyes opened, he looked around, fearful, and saw Eli, frowned, and said, "Who're you?"

"My name's Eli. I cleaned and bound your wounds. I'll fix us somethin' to eat in a bit. What happened here?"

The man struggled to breathe, squirmed a little to get comfortable, and looked at Eli, "I'm Levi Mallory. Where's muh partner?"

Eli frowned, "Dark-haired man, splotchy whiskers, scar over one eye?"

"That's Evan Donahue, muh partner. Where is he?"

"He's dead."

Levi dropped his eyes, shook his head, and muttered. He looked up to Eli, "Did they get our poke?"

"Dunno. They rode outta here in a hurry. I clipped one of 'em, maybe both. They weren't answerin' any questions."

Levi squirmed a little, trying to look behind him, but winced at the pain. He looked at Eli, "There's a box," pointing over his right shoulder, "says DuPont Blasting Powder. Our pokes are in there."

"Do you want me to look?"

"Yeah," struggled Levi, looking to Eli but frowning.

Eli stepped over the man, bent to the box, and lifted the lid. Inside were several buckskin drawstring pouches. He said, "Looks like several, uh, 'bout ten pouches here."

Levi slowly nodded, "Good, good. You musta chased 'em off 'fore they got to it. Thanks, thanks a lot," he mumbled.

Eli sat down next to the man, looked at him, "Uh, that chest wound you got, the bullet's still in there. Is there a sawbones in town or anywhere you know?"

"They got a fella calls himself Doc, pulls teeth an' such, but he ain't never sober. I wouldn't trust him to work on my mother-in-law, even if I had one." He paused, tried to take a deep breath but winced, shook his head, "There's a woman, half-breed Sioux, she's done some doctorin' an' such. An' there's a doc in Helena."

"Don't think I could get a doc to come all the way out here from Helena."

"We got us a wagon an' team."

"I'm no doctor, but after what I seen in the war, that bullet needs to come out of there and soon. Do you think you could stand a wagon ride to Helena?"

"Can't leave muh claim. Specially since them fellas done tried to take ever'hin'." He shook his head, "Course if'n I'm dead, reckon it won't make no difference." He frowned and a slow smile began to paint his face, "I know, Red and Blake, get one of 'em to drive me to Helena, th'other'n can watch my claim."

"What about theirs?" asked Eli.

"Ah, they ain't been gettin' much, an' if I tell 'em they can have what they get from our'n while I'm laid up, they'll jump at the chance," he chuckled.

————

ELI MADE a bed of blankets in the box of the wagon; it was a deep box Army supply wagon and there was plenty of room for the box of pokes beside Levi's head. The team was a matched pair of mules and were anxious to stretch out. With his horses tied on behind, Eli drove the wagon the short way down the road to the claim where he had coffee just that morning. The wagon road hung on the high side of Prickly Pear Creek and Eli pulled up across the creek from the claim of Red and Blake. He called over, "Hey, Red! It's Eli! I got a wounded man here. Can you come across; he wants to talk to you?"

The big man waved, grabbed his rifle, and splashed across the creek and stepped to the back of the box to look over the tailgate at Levi. "What happened, Levi?"

"Couple o' poke robbers. They kilt Evan. Eli here run 'em off and bandaged me up. He says I need to get to a doctor, but I didn't wanna leave muh claim. I got me an idee."

"An idee? What'chu thinkin'?" asked Red. Blake had joined them and stood beside his partner.

"How 'bout one o' you drivin' me to the doc in Helena, the other'n watchin' o'er muh claim?"

"What 'bout our'n?" pleaded Blake.

"If you wanna work our sluice, you can have all you take while I'm gone," declared Levi, looking from Red to Blake.

The two men looked at one another and both broke into a smile. Red leaned over the sideboard and stretched out a hand, "You got yoresef' a driver an' a claim work-er!" he declared, shaking hands with Levi.

Eli climbed down from the seat, wrapped the reins over the brake lever, and shook hands with Red. "You take care of him now, y'hear?"

"Umhmm. Say, did you find out about yore boys?"

Eli nodded, "He said he had no idea where they went, but a man had been through talkin' about Confederate Gulch. But, I'll try a few other places 'fore I go that far."

"Good luck!" he declared as he watched Eli step aboard the tall red dun and nudge him down the road, with a wave over his shoulder.

CHAPTER 20

INQUIRIES

Eli paused at the end of the street that held three saloons, a mercantile, and assay office, a barber/dentist office, a livery, and a haberdasher. It was nothing like the typical sleepy western town that was as much dust as wind-faded clapboard buildings, although that was an apt description, but this was a busy little town. One of the earliest gold finds in the valley was on the hills just above the Prickly Pear Creek, a rich vein that had bled its dust into the creek only to be found by a wandering prospector that thought he was seeing things when the sloshing water in his pan showed gold.

The streets were busy with supply wagons, pack mules, and sleepy horses that stood hipshot at hitchrails, waiting for their thirsty riders. The Three Deuces saloon had two old-timers sitting on a bench swapping lies and spitting tobacco across the boardwalk. The swinging doors seemed to keep swinging with the passing through of so many thirsty men and Eli thought it might be just the place to ask around.

He nudged Rusty to a hitchrail in front of a small storefront that advertised a gunsmith and guns. He stepped down, slapped the reins of Rusty and the lead rope of the grey around the hitchrail, and took to the boardwalk toward the entry to the Three Deuces. He neared the old-timers, who apparently were having a spitting contest, and when Eli stepped in front of them, one toothless old man whose chin almost touched his nose, choked back a mouthful of tobacco juice and glared at Eli. Eli chuckled, knowing what a struggle it was to swallow the juice and flipped a coin to the old man, "Sorry friend, here, have a drink on me!"

The old man nodded, trying to grin and breathe at the same time, as his partner said, "Whatta'bout me?"

Eli flipped another coin to the second man, "C'mon in and if you can answer some questions for me, I might buy you 'nother."

Both the old-timers scrambled to their feet and followed after Eli as he pushed through the swinging doors. He stepped to the side, letting his eyes adjust to the dim light of the interior. The window to the right of the door did little to let any light through the fly specked panes but did manage to show a shaft of sunlight with dust dancing as it lanced to the floor. Two lanterns hung on the walls, dirty reflectors valiantly trying to illumine the dark room, but failing.

The two old-timers were already at the bar, slapping their coins down and demanding a drink. Eli started to move, but the familiar sight of two men further down the bar gave him pause. A big man with a shock of red hair between his collar and his floppy felt hat made Eli frown, but the bald man with a bandage wrapped around his leg and trousers convinced him these were the two that killed Levi Mallory's partner and tried to kill him. His nostrils flared as he forced himself to calm as he walked to the bar, taking a place between the old-timers and the outlaws.

Eli nodded to the bartender for a mug of beer and stood with one foot on the brass footrail as he looked about. He turned sideways, his back to the old-timers as he lifted his mug of tepid beer and looked around at the room. Several tables had men playing poker, a keno table near the corner had two men facing the dealer, and three women were making the rounds, greeting customers and prospects. One of the old-timers tapped Eli on the shoulder, "What's them questions you had fer us? We need another drink!"

Eli motioned to the bartender to bring the men another drink and told the man, "Enjoy, we'll talk after you drink."

"Alright wit' me!" declared the man, slapping his friend on the back and leaning forward on the bar.

As Eli stood, looking around, he heard the voice of one of the women, now standing between the two outlaws, say, "You don't have enough money for me. I wouldn't go anywhere with you! You stink!" The big redhead growled and backhanded the woman, knocking her to the floor, and growled, "You'll do…" but was interrupted when Eli's beer mug crashed against the side of his head, dropping him like a rock. The big man crumpled to the floor, spilling the brass spittoon over his britches and legs, but he was unconscious as he sprawled out.

His bald-headed partner turned to Eli and shouted, "You cain't do that! He's muh partner!"

"Then you should have taught him some manners. I won't abide a man that mistreats a woman, any woman!" Eli glared at the bald man, waiting for any response and the man grabbed for the pistol in his belt, but the big Colt Army .44 in Eli's hand stared its one eye at the frantic man who started backstepping, hands held wide to his side. He stammered, "I din't mean nuthin'! But Bert ain't gonna be happy when he wakes up, he'll come lookin' fer you!" he threatened, trying to replace his fear with bluster.

Eli turned to the bartender, "You got a sheriff in this town?"

"No sir, but there are some vigilantes that take care of things."

"Then you might want to send for 'em. These two killed a man up the creek, tried to steal their pokes, and almost killed the partner. That was before they tried to kill me."

"Who'd they kill?" asked the bartender.

"Fella by the name of Evan somethin', Donahue I think. His partner is Levi Mallory. He's on his way to Helena and a doctor. Another man, Red, is taking him to Helena."

The bartender looked at the bald man who stood between the end of the bar and another window, hands stretched out to his side as he watched the pistol in Eli's hand. "You done that?" he asked.

Baldy shrugged, "We was broke, thot it'd be easy, till that fella come along."

The bartender motioned to three men that had been sitting at a table but watching and listening to what was happening. One of the men stepped forward, stood between Eli and the outlaw, and looked to the bartender. Eli heard the bartender tell the man to fetch the dentist and tell him to bring others.

Eli was distracted when the woman that had been knocked down walked to the redhead on the floor, leaned over, and spit on him. Eli chuckled and said, "I think it'll take more'n that to get rid of the stink."

The woman giggled and shook her head, "He could soak in the river till doomsday, and he'd still stink!" She smiled at Eli, "Thank you. I never had anybody take up for me like that before." She stepped closer and came between Eli and baldy, which gave the outlaw an excuse to grab his pistol and drag it from his belt. The click of the hammer cocking made Eli shoulder the woman aside and fire. The Colt bucked, spat fire, lead, and death as the bullet blossomed red on the man's chest, driving the second button into his chest and knocking the man back against and through the window.

Eli looked down to see the woman, blood coming from her shoulder and running down her chest to run between the swells of her breasts. She had been hit by the stray shot of the bald outlaw. She put her hand on her shoulder as she struggled to sit up, "An' I was gonna call you a gentleman!" she said to Eli, forcing a grin as he reached down to help her to her feet.

"Is there a doctor of any kind here?" he asked, looking from the woman to the bartender who stood at his broken window, looking at the body of the man that lay sprawled in the grass on the dirt between the buildings.

The bartender turned, hands on hips, "And we had a purty peaceful town till you came in. No, the closest thing we got to a doctor is the dentist, but he's also the barber, an' you never know if he's gonna bleed ya', pull a tooth, or cut your hair! But he's on his way. That's who I sent for."

Eli looked down at the big redhead who had not moved and nudged his foot to see if he was coming around. But there was no movement. Eli dropped down to his haunches, pushed at the man's shoulder, "Hey, hey!" he called, trying to get some response. It was then he noticed the pool of blood under his mop of red hair and felt hat that lay with hair tangled in the chin strap. He nudged him again, turned his face to him and saw sightless eyes.

Eli stood, looked to the bartender, nodded to the man on the floor, "He's dead."

The bartender shook his head, looked at one of the other men at the table, "John, go see what's keepin' the barber. He's the undertaker, too, so get him to bring his wagon so he can take these two!" He looked back to Eli, "You make this kind of mess everywhere you go?"

Eli chuckled, "No, I just came in lookin' for a couple of young men, twins. Thought maybe you'd seen them." He looked at the two old-timers who stood side by side, leaning against the bar and staring wide-eyed at Eli. "That's what I was goin' to ask you two." He dug in his pocket, brought out the tintype and handed it to the old-timers, "That's them. Have you seen 'em around? They were working for Donahue and Mallory but took off last week."

"What'chu wan'em fer?" asked the talkative one.

"They're my sons. I promised their ma I'd try to get 'em to go home."

"Nope," he handed the tintype to his partner who echoed his words and handed the tintype to the bartender.

Eli looked at the aproned man, "Seen 'em?"

The bartender shook his head, "Might have, not sure. Don't see twins that often. But, I just don't know. Get so many in here I get to where I just don't pay attention. Unless they start killin' people and bustin' windows and such. Ain't about to forget that!"

Eli dropped a twenty-dollar gold piece on the counter, nodded to the others, and walked out through the swinging doors. He stepped aboard the claybank and reined around just as a wagon with a sign on the side *Undertaker* was pulling to a stop in front of the saloon.

CHAPTER 21

QUESTIONS

The big stallion was an eye-catcher and several of the men that walked the boardwalk stopped and looked on as Eli rode past. He paid little attention to the onlookers but was himself looking for any business he thought might have seen his boys. Spotting the Mercantile, he nudged Rusty and the grey to the hitchrail and stepped down. The doors stood wide open, and even the boardwalk was used to display some of the wares offered by the storekeeper. Eli stepped into the store, glanced at the shelves and countertops heavy with goods and several people crowded about, some with arms full, all with patience wearing thin as they waited their turn.

"Well, I haven't seen you around here, you new to these parts?" Eli turned to see a woman with her arms full of bolts of cloth as she waited for the storekeeper. She was middle-aged but attractive with her hair piled high in pin curls and a shiny white ribbon woven through the raven black tresses. Her dress was simple but well-made and tailored to fit as she had curves in all the right places.

Eli tipped his hat to the woman and answered, "You could say that. I've been around a few days, but not looking to stay. Hunting for someone," he explained, then nodded to her armload, "Dressmaker?"

The woman smiled, nodding, "Yes, yes I am. I make all the dresses for the *ladies* of the *Red Rooster*."

Eli frowned, "Not familiar with that."

The woman snickered a little, gave a coy smile and said, "You *are* new around here if you don't know the Red Rooster."

Eli understood, nodded, "I take it you've been here a spell?"

"Yes, but I don't work there, as I said, I am the dressmaker *only,*" she clarified with a smile.

"Then you might be just the one I need to ask," he began as he reached for the tintype. He held it for her to see and explained, "Those are my sons. I'm looking for them and thought you might have seen them. I know they were around here within the last couple weeks and, well, maybe…" he shrugged as she looked at the picture.

"Nice-looking boys, twins?"

"Yes. They're in their early twenties."

"They're your sons and you don't know how old they are?"

Eli grinned, "They're my stepsons and I wasn't around much when they were growing up, army."

The dressmaker leaned forward for a better look, and glanced from the tintype to Eli and back, "They look familiar. I think I have seen them, but, well, I dunno. I don't see many folks except here at the mercantile or at the Red Rooster. If it was there…I tell you what. Madame Beauchamp sees everyone and knows most everyone. She would be the one that could tell you if the boys were there. Now mind, I'm not saying they were there, but she might have seen them elsewhere."

"And how do I find this Madame Beauchamp?" asked Eli, getting a little hopeful for the first time in a while.

"If you will wait until I'm finished here, I will take you to her. Otherwise, she might not take the time to talk."

Eli carried the woman's packages as they left the Mercantile, but she paused just outside the door, looked up the street and said, "I was going to stop at *Mama's* for some dinner. Would you mind?" she asked, smiling coyly to Eli.

"Of course not, but how 'bout I strap these packages on my packhorse until we're done?"

"Oh yes, that will be fine," she replied, fanning herself with a little fold-up fan as she smiled at Eli, her reticule dangling from her wrist. When Eli finished with the packages, he offered his arm, and she gladly slipped her hand through and moved closer to him as they walked on the boardwalk.

She led the way into the café and to a table near the window. Eli pulled out the chair for her, seated her, and took the chair to her left with his back to the window. An apron-clad woman came to the table with a coffeepot and greeted them with a smile, "Good evening, Margaret. How are you this evening?"

"Oh, fine Marylou, just fine. Marylou," she began, turning to Eli, "this is my friend," and realized she did not know his name and looked askance to him.

Eli nodded, "Eli, Eli McCain, ma'am. Pleased to meet you."

"And you, too, Eli." She smiled at Margaret, asked, "Are you eating, or just having coffee?"

Margaret looked at Eli, and he said, "We'll be eating. Do you have a special?"

"Yes, steak and potatoes. Two servings?"

"Beef?" asked Eli, surprised.

"Yes, it's part of the herd that came up from Texas," she smiled, pleased to know something others did not. The first trail drive to make it to Montana Territory had made news and hers had been one of the few dining places to get some of the beef.

"Then yes, we'll have two orders," answered Eli. He looked at Margaret, smiling, "I know there were cattle in Montana before, some of the early ranchers had some shorthorns, but I heard about a drive of Longhorns coming up from Texas, a fella by the name of Nelson Story, I believe."

The two had just finished their meal and sat back to enjoy another cup of coffee when Margaret looked up to see two women coming into the crowded café. She waved them over to the table, offered the two empty seats and introduced Eli. "Ladies, this is my friend, Eli McCain. Eli this is Madame—or Mamie—Beauchamp and Gigi Fournier."

Eli stood, helped the ladies be seated and sat down as he said, "Very pleased to meet you ladies."

Margaret waited until Marylou took the ladies' orders then leaned forward slightly, "Mamie, Eli is looking for his sons, twins. I told him you might have seen them and with your excellent memory, you would certainly know." She turned to Eli, "Show her the tintype, Eli."

Eli grinned, dug in his pocket for the tintype and handed it to Mamie, who accepted it with a smile and a nod, and leaned closer to Gigi so they both could look at it. She smiled, glanced up to Eli, "They are good-looking boys, but they don't resemble you."

"They were fortunate to take after their mother. But I'm their stepfather. I made the promise to their mother to try and find them. She was hopeful they would return home."

"Oh, I see. Then they're not in any trouble?"

"Not that I know of, no. They did leave the army, the war, without permission, but that's in the past. And their last letter said they were coming to the goldfields. I tracked them to a claim held by Evan Donahue and Levi Mallory, but they left there a week or so back."

"And what did Levi and Evan tell you about them?" asked Mamie. It was obvious she knew the two prospectors as she smiled at Eli, expecting some revelation about the boys.

"Levi didn't say much, only that they left, but he did say the boys had talked to a couple men that passed through who told them about Confederate Gulch. Levi thought they might have gone there."

"What about Evan?"

"Nothing. He couldn't. He had been killed by a couple poke robbers that hit them just before I got there. But Levi survived and Red and Blake were taking him to Helena to a doctor."

Mamie frowned, "That's too bad. They're good men, always behaved themselves," she said as she glanced to Gigi who nodded her agreement. She looked back to Eli, "Yes, I know your boys. Joshua and Jubal, right?"

Eli was surprised, but nodded and grinned as he leaned his elbows on the table to look at Mamie. "I met them in here, at that table over there," nodding to another table that sat in front of the big window. "They were very mannerly, and we talked a while. I had heard them discussing different places to go and when we talked, I shared with them what little I knew and had often wondered about."

Eli frowned, "And what was that?"

She smiled, "I hear men talk all the time about the dust they pan from the creeks, a few that try digging a little and using their sluice boxes, and none of 'em seem to have enough sense to wonder where the gold comes from. Common sense would tell you it gets washed down the streams from somewhere higher up, so I asked the boys, 'Why don't you pan your way to the source?' you know, where it comes from. Logic says, you keep panning while you get color, then when there is no more color, you look for the original source. It's probably further up the mountain! I had one of the most successful prospectors explain that to me and he just echoed what I had been thinking all along. So, I asked the boys about it." She smiled as she looked around the table.

Margaret looked at her friend and asked, "Well, what happened? What'd they do?"

"They said that's what they had thought about since they were getting good gold for Evan and Levi. But they didn't have enough money to supply their looking, so..." she smiled as she looked around the table again, "I staked 'em!"

"You staked them?" asked Eli, frowning.

"That's right. I've done it before, usually pays off too. They said they would go upstream of where they were working on the Prickly Pear and do just as I suggested and hopefully find the mother lode! If they do, it'll be a good 'un!" she declared, smiling.

CHAPTER 22

TRAIL

B oth horses were eye catchers; Josh rode a dark bay with black legs, mane, and tail and Jubal had a blood sorrel with a white diamond on his face and front legs with stockings. Both horses had the body build of a quarter horse, broad chest, powerful rounded hindquarters, and the well-shaped head with soft eyes and an arched neck of the Morgan. The geldings were both crossbred Quarter-Morgan product of the ancestral home horse ranch in Louisville, Kentucky, where the twins spent their growing-up years. When they deserted the army, their grandmother outfitted them with horses, tack and a bag of money, reflective of her views of the war. Now they rode the trail that sided the Prickly Pear Creek that ultimately fed into the Missouri River, and were bound for the mountains that might prove to be the source of the gold that other miners were washing from the creek bed.

Jubal, being the more impulsive of the twins, was quick to accept the grubstake offer from Madame Beauchamp, even though they had squirreled away enough high-graded dust and nuggets to outfit themselves. They also had a pouch of gold coins that their grandmother had stashed away in their saddlebags without telling them. It wasn't until they were checking their gear and stashing their high-grade before leaving Montana City that Joshua found it, choosing to keep it as an emergency fund and not tell Jubal.

The grubstake provided enough for them to outfit themselves with shovels, pans, tools, a wall tent, and a good supply of foodstuffs, to load in their new panniers aboard the new pack mule they dubbed Meg. Jubal was in the lead, keeping to the high side of the wagon road away from the creek. With many working claims on the creek, they hailed most of the miners as they passed, but as they neared the claim of Mallory and Donahue, Jubal took a game trail that rode the shoulder on the east side of the creek and kept to the black timber. They had not left the claim they worked on the best of terms, leaving in the night to avoid any confrontations, and now chose to avoid any possible conflict.

As they neared a bit of a clearing where the trees were sparse, Jubal stopped, stepped down and walked into the open to look below at the claim where they had worked and learned. He frowned as he watched one man, a big man with a shock of red hair, working at the sluice. There was no one else within sight, and Jubal motioned to Joshua to join him. He nodded to the claim, "That's not Levi or Evan. Who d'ya s'pose that is?"

Joshua watched the worker, who knew the workings of a sluice and was washing a lot of gravel. "That looks like Red, from the camp just below theirs."

"But, what's he doin' workin' their claim?" asked Jubal, even though Joshua knew nothing more about the claim. He looked at his brother, "What say we go down an' ask?"

"Yeah, somethin' ain't right."

They cut through the big ponderosa and fir, their animals moving almost noiselessly as they stepped on the needle-carpeted hillside. When they dropped from the trail onto the wagon road, they pushed across the creek and came into the camp with a "Hello the camp! We're comin' in and we're friendly!" and approached slowly with hands lifted to show they were not holding weapons.

"Wal! If'n it ain't the twins! What'chu doin' round'chere? I thought you was off findin' yore own claim?" greeted Red.

"We are, we're headin' into the high country, upstream of here, lookin' for some place without a bunch of claims," answered Jubal, leaning on the saddle horn as he looked at the big Irishman. "What're you doin' here, an' where's Levi and Evan?"

Red shook his head, stepped back from the sluice and dropped the gate so the water would flow into the creek. He looked at the boys, "They got hit by some poke thieves. Both of 'em were shot, Evan didn't make it an' muh partner took Levi into Helena to find a doctor. I'm watchin' an' workin' their claim while he's gone. Hopefully he'll make it, but I doubt it. He was hit purty bad." He shook his head, then with a grin he looked back to the boys, "If it weren't fer yore pappy, Levi wouldn'ta made it long as he done. He brought him down to our camp, convinced me'n Blake to take Levi to Helena an' watch his claim while he was gone." He chuckled as he glanced back to the sluice, "An' that long-tom shore do the work. Yessiree, I've already got more'n I woulda got in a week on our claim!"

"Hold on, hold on!" declared Jubal, lifting his hand toward Red as he looked from the big man to his brother. "Did you say, our pappy? Do you mean somebody claiming to be our father was here?"

Red grinned, chuckled, "Yup, tha's 'xactly what I was sayin'. He said he was your stepdaddy an' he was lookin' fer you. Had him a tintype of the two of you and ever'thin'."

"Big man, broad shouldered, dark hair, looks like a cavalry officer?"

Red nodded, "Ummhmm. Tha's him alright. Said he promised yore mama to bring you home!"

Jubal looked to his brother and back to Red, "When was this?"

"Couple days ago, le's see," he paused, obviously counting on his fingers and frowning as he remembered, "Yeah, maybe three days ago. I been here two days an' it was the day afore, so, yeah, 'bout three days, if'n I'm recomemberin' right."

"And all he said was about our mother, not the army?"

"Ummhmm, but the way he talked about yo' mother, well, it just din't seem quite right, like maybe she had passed or sumpin'. I dunno, mebbe it's just me bein' in the mountains too long."

"Where'd he go from here?" asked Joshua.

"I reckon he went into Montana City, leastways that's what I thought. But Levi tol' him you boys had talked to a fella 'bout Confederate Gulch and thought maybe that's where you went. So, mebbe he headed that'away," shrugged Red. He nodded to the boys, "I gotta get back to work, be seein' you!"

"Yeah. Oh, an' if you see our father, you can tell him

we went to Jefferson City. Gonna start lookin' past there."

Red nodded, turned away with a wave over his shoulder and opened the floodgate on the sluice to return to his work. With a glance to Joshua, Jubal led them from the camp and took to the wagon road south to go deeper into the mountains.

The furthest upstream from the Donahue-Mallory claim the two brothers had been, was the second creek from the west, some were already calling it Clancy Creek. Both Buffalo Creek and Clancy Creek had claims near the confluence of the creeks with Prickly Pear Creek, but as far as they could see, there were no other claims upstream from those. Jubal looked to Joshua, "Whadaya think? Should we try those?"

"Nah, if there was much there, I think there'd already be more claims. If these at the mouth of the creeks aren't doin' much, and we can tell that cuz both those fellas are just usin' rockers, then there'd be more claims upstream. Let's keep goin' and when we get to a place where we can give it a try, let's do a few pans, see if we get color."

Jubal nodded, knowing his brother was the thinker of the two and he trusted his judgment. He nudged his sorrel gelding forward, pulling on the lead of the mule, and resumed his pace on the wagon road. The meandering Prickly Pear Creek had been hugging the hillside to the east but cut across the narrow valley to slip into the shadow of the west slopes that showed thick and tall timber. Laced with ponderosa with long needles that showed like thick hair standing tall over the often-shorter fir and spruce, the black timber rose high above the cottonwoods, willows, and aspen that followed the water.

When the creek cut across the wagon road, a gravelly

bottomed crossing invited travelers to split the willows and cross. Jubal reined up at the stream, stepped down and let the horses and mule have a drink. He arched his back as he watched the animals, and Joshua stood at creek side, staring down into the crystal clear water, searching for any glitter that might hold promises. But their attention was arrested when a rattle of gunfire split the silence, bouncing across the narrow vale and echoing back to multiply the ruckus. The horses and mule lifted their heads, ears pricked, and Jubal swung aboard as he hollered to his brother, "Let's take cover in the trees!"

The sorrel jumped into the water as soon as Jubal hit the seat, and the bay of Joshua was close on his heels, but Joshua had not gotten a foot in the stirrup, but he grabbed the saddle horn and hung on as the gelding splashed water to cross the creek. As soon as the bay's feet hit solid dirt, he stretched out, and Joshua dug heels in the dirt, the momentum carrying his legs up as he swung his feet over the rump of the horse and landed in the saddle. Jubal took to the trees, driving through the thickets, head down as limbs slapped at him, but the sorrel drove on. Within moments, Jubal reined up, the trees thinning enough they could stand easy, and they listened, hearing the heavy breathing of the horses and mule, as they waited, wondering what the rattle of gunfire could portend. Jubal looked at Joshua, "Wouldn't been hunters—too much shooting."

"Unless they ran into a herd of buffalo or elk or somethin'," suggested Joshua.

"Nah, I don't think so. It was too fast, too close together. It was more like a gunfight."

"That could only mean claim jumpers or poke thieves."

"Yeah," mumbled Jubal, cocking his head to the side,

listening. He stepped down, stroked the sorrel's neck, calming the horse as he continued to listen. When the gelding's head lifted, ears pricked, and turned toward the stream below them, they heard the clatter of horse hooves.

"That's somebody, several riders, moving fast," said Jubal.

"That can't be good. If it's the thieves, they're makin' their getaway, an' if it's the claim owners, they're tryin' to get away."

"Sounds to me like it's a good time to give the horses a break, let 'em enjoy some o' this grass. We got a couple cans o' peaches that are callin' my name. How 'bout'chu?"

Joshua grinned, "I could eat some peaches," as he stepped down and dropped the reins to ground tie the horse. He looked at his brother and asked, "So, what about our father?"

"Yeah, what about him?" asked Jubal, shaking his head. "And what about Mom? Red seemed to think the way Dad talked, she had passed."

"We need to get a letter off to her, maybe she can write back and fill us in on what the old man is doing. If he's still Army, he might be lookin' for deserters."

Jubal shook his head, "I thought about that, but…" he shrugged, "I just don't see him doin' that. If he did, Ma would have his head for sure!"

Josh chuckled, "Yeah she would. She never liked the idea of us joinin' up anyway, and Gramma, well, you know how she felt."

Jubal grinned, leaned back as he opened the can of peaches with his knife, "Gramma was somethin', wasn't she?"

"Yeah. It woulda been good if we coulda gone back

after she passed, but…" he shrugged, thinking of the penalty for desertion.

The two savored the unusual treat of canned peaches and stretched out in the shade for a short nap, letting the animals graze on the greenery in the little clearing. They trusted the horses to alert them if there was any danger of visitors and knew they could snooze safely.

CHAPTER 23

EXPLORE

The hotel was more of a tent than a building. Although the false front gave it the appearance of a two-story building, it was nothing more than a pretense to draw in the gold-blinded prospectors and any others that could be taken. The narrow structure held a counter, waiting room, and a front door. Eli had taken a cot and spent a restless night, thinking about his boys and how close he had been to finding them, but he had hope he would soon catch up to them and tell them about their mother. He rolled to his side, trying to stifle the sound of so many snoring men and the stench of so many unwashed bodies, all the while wishing he had already stocked up and could be sleeping under the stars with an abundance of fresh air.

All his efforts at sleep proved useless, prompting Eli to rise from the cot, gather his gear and start from the canvas hotel while the stars still shone. He had put Rusty and the grey in the livery and wished he had stayed with them; the loft would have offered better rest than the hotel. Rusty craned his neck around to see Eli drag the saddle from the fence and appeared to roll his eyes, stretch his head out and flap his lips as if he was protesting the early rise. When both horses were rigged up, Eli led them from the livery, and with the muted pinks of early morning showing beyond the low hills, he mounted up and started from the little town.

The road pointed south, with faded layers of hills poking their noses through the morning mist and haze. The dim wagon road that pointed south to follow the Prickly Pear Creek split two hills, one anthill-looking bald knob that rose about three hundred feet above the road, while on the west side, another similar hill with timber on its north face, rose about a hundred feet higher. The creek sided the wagon road between the two buttes and lay low on the west side, twisting through the willows and alders.

Eli heard riders coming, and moved to the right edge of the road, making room for the others. Three riders showed as the road bent around a shoulder of the timber-covered hills. A big man led the trio and as he neared, Eli's first thought was the man had a face that looked like a potato that had been dragged behind a wagon in a sack. The man's nose bent two directions, probably the result of several fights, his face was pock-marked and scarred. Black eyes, filled with scorn and contempt, glared from under a forehead heavy with thick eyebrows. A black hat shaded his face, broad shoulders spread from a tree stump neck. Eli had the impression a big beer barrel was riding the saddle.

Beside the leader and slightly behind him, the second man who appeared to be just as tall, a thin man with a face that showed careless and mean, evoked evil as the young man sneered at the passerby, even to curling his lip in contempt. The third man was an Indian, or at least a half-breed, that wore his hair in the fashion of the Natives, long braids that trailed down his back. A beaded headband held a pair of feathers, both pointing down, at the back of his head. A leather vest, beaded, showed a bare chest and arms, and fringed britches topped beaded moccasins. The Indian did not look at Eli, but kept his attention on the road ahead, following close behind the others.

Eli nodded as they passed, receiving no acknowledgement from the others. Eli kept riding, did not look after the three, knowing they were trouble. As the dust in the road settled after the men had passed, Eli breathed deep of the pine scent, the clear air invigorating. He grinned to himself, *Eli, you're beginning to act like some old hermit. Can't seem to stand bein' around people, but always mixin' up in their business.*

He passed the claim of Red and Blake, noticing no sign of life, no sign of recent working or moving about. He lifted his eyes past the creek to the terrain on the right where rolling hills showed some timber on the north-facing slopes with a bigger hill showing a black face to the north. To his left, taller timber-covered hills stood in the shadow of big mountains that held mystery and promise. As he neared the camp of Donahue and Mallory, Eli expected to see the big Irishman, Red, working at the sluice. As he pushed across the creek, he saw the camp was in disarray, the sluice with its props knocked out, showed nothing but the cascade of water splashing over the debris. The two wall tents had also been pulled down, tools, boxes, and more were scattered about. Eli saw the big hobnailed boots showing from the canvas of what had been the sleeping tent. Eli stopped, looked around, stood in his stirrups and looked downstream to the wagon road and the hillsides. Nothing moved except a lone eagle drifting on the morning breeze as he looked for his next prey.

Eli stepped down, dropped the reins to ground tie the claybank stallion and went to the trashed tent where Red lay. He pulled away the canvas and saw the bloodied remains of Red. He had been shot, beaten, and dragged. Whoever raided the camp must have thought there should be more gold than what Red had and tortured him for the whereabouts of the stash, but Red could not, nor would not, tell them, even if he could. His stubborn Irish nature sealed his fate. Eli shook his head, dragged the body from the tent and scrounged up a shovel and began to dig a grave next to the grave of Evan Donahue.

Eli was soon back on the road south. He believed the perpetrators of the murder of Red were the three that he passed leaving town. But he was not the law, and he was closer to finding his boys than he had been, and he was bound to fulfill the promise before anything else. It's not that he wanted to neglect what had become his mantra, to always help others when you can and never let evil go unpunished, but he had to find the twins. He took a deep breath that lifted his shoulders and dropped his eyes to the road, intent on fulfilling the covenant he made with his wife.

Eli soon began to see a pattern. Every claim that was somewhat isolated, had been hit and the miner killed, camp ransacked and nothing of value left behind. Horses and mules and heavy gear remained. After burying the one man from the first claim above Red's grave, he stayed on the road and looked at the scenes from a distance. Whenever there were several claims together, usually at the confluence of creeks, nothing had happened and the miners were all busy with their rockers, panning, and more. Most waved as Eli passed, returning the wave and/or shouted greetings, and if the road was close enough, Eli shared what had happened to the other claim holders.

One man stood, leaving his pan in the water, and with thumbs behind his braces, he spat a chaw of tobacco, wiped his chin, "You know, I saw them fellers, had muh rifle right handy and watched 'em. They looked right bad, they did. Wouldn't turn muh back on 'em, nosirree."

Eli described the three he saw at first light and the man replied, "Yup. That was them aw'right. Bad'uns."

"You're smart in keeping your rifle handy, but if you get a chance to pass the word to others, do it."

"I will, yessir, you can count on that! An' thanks fer tellin' us!" he declared, nodding to Eli and glancing back to his partner who had stayed at his work, washing another pan full of gravel.

It was less than ten miles from the burial of Red to the settlement of Jefferson City, and in that distance, Eli had seen at least five claims that had been raided by the outlaws. As he rode into the small town that lay in a vale below the rugged foothills, one main street and a few scattered cabins were nestled into the little flats beside Prickly Pear Creek and between Dutchman Creek and Spring Creek. A small clapboard building with a porch over the boardwalk showed a sign that simply stated, *Sheriff*.

Eli nudged Rusty to the hitchrail, pulled on the lead of the grey and slid to the ground to tie them both off. He stepped up on the boardwalk just as a badge-wearing handlebar moustache stepped from the office, "Howdy, stranger!" he declared, one hand resting on the butt of his holstered pistol and the other twisting the end of his whiskers.

Eli stopped, frowned, and with a grin, held out his hand, "Howdy, Sheriff. I'm Eli McCain."

The man shook hands with Eli, nodding and grinning, "What brings you to our little town, Eli?"

Eli dug in his pocket to retrieve the tintype, "I'm looking for my two boys. Jubal and Joshua Paine."

The sheriff looked at the tintype, frowning, "Thot you said yore name was McCain?"

"That's right. They're my stepsons."

The sheriff slowly lifted his head as he handed back the tintype, "Don't recall seein' 'em. What'chu wan' 'em fer?"

"I promised their mother I'd find them, try to get them to go home."

"There's a lotta women that'd like that of their men and their boys."

"Ummhmm. Also, I just came up from Montana City. Passed about a half-dozen claims that had been hit by outlaws. They killed the claim owners, took anything of value, and kept going. I passed three men that looked like they might be the ones that did it, but I don't know for sure. One man on a claim they didn't hit remembered them passing and thought they were trouble, had a rifle handy and showed it."

"What'd they look like?"

Eli took the time to describe the three down to the horses they rode and the clothes they wore. "I buried a couple of the prospectors, but by the time I came on the third one, I thought I might do better by telling the others about the problem. I wasn't sure it was those men I saw and thought they might be heading this way, so…" he shrugged.

"Wal, it's a bad thing what happened, but that ain't

my jurisdiction. I'm a local sheriff, just concerned 'bout things hereabouts."

"Maybe you could send word to the sheriff in Helena or maybe the vigilantes?"

"Wal, if'n I know somebody goin' that way, I might just do that. Right now, I'm goin' to git me some vittles."

"That's where I was headed too. What do you recommend?"

"Only place in town is Coffee John's Chop House. Best and worst we got, but it's all we got!" he chuckled. "Join me!"

Eli chuckled, "I'll just do that, thank you."

CHAPTER 24

THREATS

The sheriff was a round shouldered man, a touch of grey in his moustache and thinning hair betrayed his age, but Eli was certain he wasn't as old as his wrinkled face showed. He was what some might call weather beaten, not unlike the paint peeling hot sun faded buildings that lined the street of Jefferson City. But he was not a man to be lightly considered, the glint in his eyes seemed to say that he already knew what you were thinking and was about two or three steps ahead. His was the type of man that opened territories, exploring country where no white man had been before and befriending Natives that others feared. And he prevailed, what some would call a curly old codger.

The sheriff was friendly with the matronly woman that came to their table with a hot coffeepot and a wide smile. As she pushed a wayward tuft of hair from her face, she poured the coffee and asked, "So, Reuben, what'll it be?"

The sheriff smiled at the woman in a way that told of

a special friendship as she stood close to him, leaning on his shoulder with her hip, "What'chu got, Amy?"

"Same as always, Reuben. Some kinda stew, biscuits, coffee. But…" she paused and smiled at him special, "I made a pie from them apples you had in your cellar."

The sheriff answered, "Then we'll both have the usual, and I might even share a piece of that pie with my friend here, Eli."

Amy smiled at Eli, nodded, and looked back to the sheriff. "He an old friend?"

The sheriff grinned at Eli, looked back to Amy, "Wal, he's old and I'm thinkin' he might be a friend, so, yeah."

Amy shook her head as she chuckled and walked back to the kitchen area to fill their orders. Eli looked at the sheriff, "So, it's Reuben?"

The sheriff cocked one eyebrow up and answered, "That's right. Reuben Posthelwaite. Been here since the town's foundin' and hunted and trapped this area 'fore anybody found gold and brought all these pilgrims in to spoil the country."

"So, did you spend any time with the Natives?"

"Yup, spent a couple winters with the Absaroka. Got to know 'em purty good, even learned a mite of their tongue."

"What do you hear about the treaty and such with Red Cloud?" asked Eli, leaning forward to reach for his coffee.

Reuben dropped his eyes as his eyebrows lifted and gave a slight shake of his head, "Wal, what I hear lately, Red Cloud's got himself a war goin'. Accordin' to what Wolf Bow told me, they was down to Fort Laramie to negotiate a treaty 'bout the Bozeman Trail that was bein' used by all these gold hunters comin' through Indian country and stakin' their claims up here, but some colonel name o' Carrington came marchin' in with over a thousand troops, couple hunnert wagons, some cannon. He said he'd come to build forts all along the Bozeman Trail to protect all them gold hunters and settlers, and he had him an attitude that didn't suit Red Cloud, so him and Young Man Afraid of his Horses and a bunch o' others, stood up from the negotiations, scowled at the soldiers, and left."

"Carrington, huh. I'm surprised they'd send a bureaucrat out west. He was never in the fight during the war, but I heard of him as some special recruiter who mustered in a bunch of troops from Ohio, the 18th Infantry, I believe it was, but he didn't get in the fight with 'em. Last I heard he had somethin' to do with the intelligence branch. But what you say doesn't surprise me, most of those appointed officers like to make a parade of just about everything. I could see him leading the parade of all those troops into the fort just to show how important he was."

"You was in the war?" asked the sheriff.

"Yeah, also spent some time in Fort Laramie before the war. Served with Sherman, cavalry, lieutenant colonel," offered Eli, keeping his explanation to a minimum. "What has Red Cloud done since?"

The sheriff sipped his coffee and Amy sat the plates of stew before them. He smiled up at her as she leaned against him, "Don't forget the pie!" he declared.

"You clean your plate first, mister!" the woman sternly replied, struggling to keep from smiling at the sheriff.

After she left the table, the men went to work on their stew, spoke little while they ate, but when Reuben wiped his plate with the last of his biscuit, he washed it down with coffee and leaned back in his chair. "You asked what Red Cloud was doin'?"

Eli nodded, his mouth full of stew as he mopped his plate with a biscuit.

"Half Yellow Face and his friend, White Swan, was through here just yestiddy." He paused and sipped some more coffee.

Eli almost choked on his coffee, "Half Yellow Face?"

The sheriff frowned, "Yeah, why?"

"He's a friend of mine. We spent some time together when I was at Fort Laramie. He taught me the ways of the woods."

"You don't say!" grinned Reuben. "Wal, ain't that sumpin'?" he chuckled. "Wal, he told me that Red Cloud had him 'bout five hunnert warriors and a couple Cheyenne, Dull Knife and Two Moons tried to make peace with Carrington down to Fort Reno. While they was talkin', Red Cloud's men stampeded the troops' horses and mules, and after the soldier boys gave chase, they kilt a handful of 'em. What them soldier boys didn't know—Red Cloud left some o' his men behind and they hit the fort and kilt 'bout a half dozen traders. After that, Red Cloud attacked a wagon train of soldiers at Crazy Woman Creek where it runs into the Powder, shed some blood there too."

"Well, at least that's well south of here," surmised Eli, draining the last of his coffee.

"Don't you believe it. What they're doin' has the Absaroka upset. They've always been enemies of the Lakota and it was the Lakota that moved 'em off their traditional hunting grounds. Now with them fightin' the white man, the Absaroka are expectin' 'em to come north and fight them. And the Blackfoot, both the Siksika and the Piikani, are getting restless. They've never been too friendly with the whites, and according to what Half Yellow Face says, he's heard the Blackfoot might move against the Absaroka or even go south against the white man." He paused, looked at Eli, and continued.

"This land," waving a hand to the mountains west of the town, "is Blackfoot territory. And right here, but south and east over beyond the Musselshell, well, that's Absaroka. We're close enough to the land of the Absaroka that they stop in here ever now'n again to get supplies and whatnot. But the Natives don't see boundaries like the white man. They believe their land is wherever they are and whatever they can keep."

Eli frowned, slowly shook his head, "And that," nodding to the west, "is where I think my boys went. They got a grubstake from the woman at the Red Rooster, and she suggested they go to the mountains and try to find the mother lode from where all the gold dust is washed downstream. She said they were quite excited about the idea and even got her excited with their enthusiasm. You know how it is with young men, always willing to chase a dream."

"They might be headin' into trouble," suggested Reuben, looking at Eli with a touch of concern showing in his grey eyes. "But I know that country. Might be I could give you an idee where you might go and mebbe stay out of trouble."

Eli chuckled, "Lately, it seems that no matter how hard I try to stay out of trouble, it seems to find me anyway."

The sheriff rose to his feet, looked at Eli, "Whyn'tchu come with me. I got me some gov'mnt maps back at the office. They ain't much good, but it'll be a startin' place. Since you're goin' into the den of the devil, might wanna know all you can."

Eli frowned at his expression, but he had heard worse about the Blackfoot people. Not that they were evil, but they had always been a fearsome warrior people and had never backed down from any other people, the white man included. He had heard tales from mountain men like Twofer, who he met on the riverboat trip from St. Louis, that always spoke of the formidable fighters of the Blackfoot. He had yet to meet anyone that had befriended them. Even Chaplain Haney, who thought he would be a part of a mission to the Blackfoot, was warned away and had chosen to join a growing work in Helena.

As they walked back to the sheriff's office, Reuben pointed out some of the landmarks of the mountains that would help him as he searched the area for his sons. He listened to what Reuben said, but his mind also traveled to his sons and the danger they were facing. They would be no different than anyone that had never spent time with Natives, and especially going into the land of the Blackfoot. He mumbled a silent prayer for his sons as he let his eyes travel across the timbered hills that rose against the sky, peaceful looking, but hiding all manner of danger to what most men like Reuben would call, greenhorns.

CHAPTER 25

NATIVES

Most of the afternoon was spent with Reuben walking around the outside of the office, pointing out landmarks to Eli, looking at the maps, and talking about the way of the Natives. "Now, as you know, just cuz some o' the villagers are friendly and ain't got nuthin' 'gainst whites, don't mean they all think that way. The Siksika band of the Blackfoot Confederacy has been peaceable, but not friendly. And there's been a time or two they had 'em a village up at the head of that draw, layin' in the shadow of the big stone fronted peak called Crow Peak." He paused, spat a gob of tobacco juice, wiped the ends of his moustache, and added, "Some o' them young bucks, wal, they just wanna count coup, take scalps, and earn honors and they ain't too partic'lar how they do it. To their way o' thinkin' as white man's scalp ain't no different from a Absaroka scalp or any of the other tribes that have been their enemy fer a long time."

"So, what you're sayin' is the boys could run into a

peaceful bunch or a band that wants their scalps and they wouldn't know the difference."

"Ummhmm," nodded the sheriff.

"And I'm not sure where to start. When they were told to go to the mountains, that could be just about anywhere."

"Ummhmm, but if I was a young'un an' wantin' to spread muh wings, an' somebody tol' me to go to the mountains, I'd go to the closest ones," he motioned to the range that lay to the east of the creek across the road from his office. "Now, if'n it were me, I think I'd ride up to the headwaters of Prickly Pear Creek, that would be the logical place, what with all the claims downstream from there. And that creek turns to the east just yonder," he pointed northwest of the town, across the road, to a coulee that cut its way from the high country. "Thataway, if'n you don't find 'em on the crick, you're in the high country an' it's easier to make your way north, with a few side runs down any crick that shows promise. Also, it's easier to see camp smoke from high up."

Eli looked at the sheriff, "Reuben, I'm mighty grateful for your help. At least now I have some direction to my wanderings and searching. I need to top off my supplies, so, I'll do that and how 'bout I meet you back to the chop house and I'll buy your supper?"

The sheriff grinned, nodded, extended his hand, "I'll do that, yesirree, I'll do that. See ya' directly!"

He stocked up at the small general store, was pleased they had ample ammunition for his many weapons, and with a fresh supply of coffee to boot, he thought he was well stocked for his foray into the mountains. His dinner with the sheriff at the familiar Coffee John's Chop House was a pleasant interlude but he left the sheriff to endure the flirtations of Amy and bid his goodbye.

A short way out of the little village, he pushed across the Prickly Pear Creek and found a grassy knoll in the thick cottonwoods and made his camp by the dim light of dusk. He rolled out his blankets, built the makings of a campfire, filled the coffee pot with fresh water, sat the bag of Arbuckles beside the rock, and looked around. All he would need to do in the morning would be to light the fire, set the pot near, saddle the horses and after his morning coffee, he would be ready to take to the hunt.

———

THE SUN WAS STILL HIDING, and the big mountains loomed like giant shadows before him. The hooves of Rusty and the grey clattered as they crossed the dusty wagon road to take the trail that sided Prickly Pear Creek. The waters chuckled over the rocks as it twisted its way among the thickets of willows and grasses of the narrow coulee. Skinny fir stretched high into the early morning darkness with random cottonwood and aspen waving their leaves at the lonely passerby. On his right, the creek talked back as the waters cascaded over the rocks and the low hills beyond matched the skeletal firs with the few retreating stars. Above him off his left shoulder, ponderosa spread their branches and waved long needles in the early morning breeze, whispering back to the rest of the skinnier trees as they too, whispered with the breeze. The mountains were talking to Eli, and he was listening, but he was also talking to his Lord, asking for guidance and success in his hunt for his boys. He added a postscript, *And Lord, keep 'em safe. They don't know what they're doin' here in Indian country, and I'd hate to find 'em too late.*

After the first mile, the valley pushed the shoulders of

the hills back and offered a wide park sloping off the hills on his left into a wide clearing with a couple random ponderosa standing in the middle, bunchgrass littered the higher slope, and gramma and Indian grass slid down to the willows. He pushed on, always watchful for any sign of others that had taken this trail recently, but all he saw was the two-toed tracks of deer and plenty of them. Another mile and the trail bent around the point of a shoulder, to break into another meadow that showed sign of elk beds.

A tall spruce showed the claw marks of a big boar grizzly, higher on the tree than Eli could reach while standing in his stirrups. He looked down at Rusty who had craned his head around to see what Eli was doing, "That is a big bear. We don't wanna run into him, boy." But the marks already showed grey, and he knew they were at least a week, probably much more, old and they were not in any immediate danger.

What had been a creek, dwindled to a trickle, small pools held enough water for game to drink, another small creek merged with the Prickly Pear, but even the two together were not big enough to make Eli have to stretch to step over. With a quick look around, he nudged Rusty to take to the trail that now moved up the shoulder and into the trees. He guessed this to be a trail of the ancients, perhaps the Blackfoot or even the Ktunaxa or Gros Ventre, *Gut People,* that were here before the Piikani. But the only recent sign was from elk, bulls rubbing their antlers on the trees to rid them of the spring velvet. Their big, splayed hooves kicked aside the long needles of the ponderosa, and their smell was on the trees. It wasn't time for the rut so he heard no bugles, but this was their domain.

As the trail approached a timber-covered bench, Eli

saw a rimrock canyon that broke off to the south with black rock and talus slopes that marred the east face, but the thick timber in the bottom offered no water or visible trails and he kept to the trail that crossed the bench. When he rounded a shoulder on his left, the hills rose steeply with mountain mahogany and some bristlecone pine atop the high ridges.

The trail dropped to the valley bottom and pushed through the trees and occasional growths of aspen. A long series of talus slopes fell from the steep ridge on the left, leaving basaltic rock barren of any greenery. Near the end of the talus slopes, the hillside receded, leaving a bald face with grassy slopes that appeared to push back the pines. Although the trail stayed just inside the tree line, he could see a sizable herd of elk lazily grazing in the warm morning sun. Orange calves frolicked about their mothers, often jamming their noses into the udder and receiving a kick from their mother's rear hoof. The cows numbered in the dozens, last year's yearlings sprouting long spikes with strips of velvet hanging were sparring near the trees, but no herd bulls were seen.

Eli reined up and leaned on the pommel of his saddle, enjoying the moment, watching the herd as it meandered about, looking for the tastiest bits of new growth grasses. Rusty and the grey were also watching the many wapiti until the head of the herd cow came up, and she sounded a grunt to warn the others and the herd moved as one, long legs stretching out as the herd scrambled for the trees higher up the slope. As Eli watched, he saw two cows stumble and fall, another one stumble, but regain its footing and stagger a little further and nose down in the grass. None of the downed cows appeared to have calves, and the rest of the herd disappeared into the thicker trees higher up the hillside.

There had been no gunshots, but Eli waited, knowing the hunters would soon show themselves and at least five men, all Natives with bare arms and chests, feathers in their hair, came from the trees, leading horses and talking loudly with one another, waving their bows in the air, rejoicing in the successful hunt. Eli sat watching, reached down to calm his big stallion and pulled the grey close beside him to talk softly to both. As the Natives began dressing out the downed elk, Eli stepped down, drew the horses into the thicker timber, and let them scrounge for some graze as they waited. He stood behind the trunk of a big ponderosa, watching as the small band of hunters did their work.

As he watched, he became engrossed in their work, paying little attention to the horses, but when Rusty brought his head up, ears pricked and looking behind Eli, Eli dropped to one knee drawing his pistol as he turned and saw an old man, standing with arms crossed, the shadows of the trees falling across him, but he stood unmoving. A slight grin parted his face and he slowly nodded, lowered his arms and came a little closer. Eli stood, holstered his Colt and greeted the man, using sign and what little he was told by Reuben. "*Okii, Nitanikkoo* Eli."

The old man grinned, "*Nitanikkoo Astsista-Mahkan.* Running Rabbit in your tongue."

Eli grinned, "So, you speak the tongue of the *Naapikoan*, white people."

The old man nodded, grinned, "You have coffee?"

"I do," declared Eli. He went to the grey, pulled out the coffeepot and the bag of Arbuckles. When he turned, he saw the old man was already laying a campfire between a couple rocks and motioned to Eli to light the fire.

Eli stepped close, dropped to one knee and gathered a handful of dry pine needles, stuffed them under the dry broken branches laid in by the old man and lit them with a lucifer. When the flame caught, the needles flared, the fire licking at the dry wood, and soon the little fire was ready for the coffeepot. Eli had filled the pot with his water bag and now sat it beside the fire. The old man had seated himself, legs crossed and arms dangling over his legs.

Eli seated himself in a similar fashion, and asked, "Are you Blackfoot, Siksika?"

The old man nodded, "Piikani. *Miaawaahpittsiiksi*, Never Lonesome clan."

Eli nodded, "My full name is Elijah McCain. I am in these mountains searching for my sons. Twins, that are looking for gold."

The old man nodded, grinned, and said, "I have watched you. I could tell you were searching for something." He looked at the coffeepot as it began to dance and motioned for Eli to put the coffee in, motioning he was anxious to drink some of the white man's coffee.

Eli grinned and complied, he was happy to be visiting with the man and was hopeful he would learn something about his boys, but he also knew he could not rush this man. The Native people are a patient people, and to rush into a conversation is considered rude. Eli sat back, waiting as patiently as he was able.

CHAPTER 26

HOPE

D utchman Creek was like so many others, its origins were high in the mountains and began with some little spring-fed pool that was the result of ground water from spring snows. When thaw came in the warm weather, the usually dry creek bed swelled with runoff from high-country snow, that runoff cascading over talus slides, rock falls, and shifting ground that usually changed the course of the creek every spring. The headwaters of Dutchman Creek were high in the Elkhorn Mountains, originating in the cradle of granite slide-rock that showed orange lichen and blue-green moss. It was in this kind of rock that Jubal and Joshua had high hopes of finding the mother lode of gold that was the source of washed down dust.

The climb to the high country had been a challenge, with the last mile or so of the trail that hugged the little creek bed thick with the mountain moss-covered slide-rock that was precarious to try to cross. The game trail they followed kept to the trees and provided them cover. They were in the black timber walking and leading the animals, giving the men a break from the saddles and the horses from carrying the weight up the steeper reaches of the trail, when Jubal hissed and held a hand behind him to stop his brother. Jubal dropped to one knee, peering under the low branches of the high-country spruce, watching the movement that had caught his eye.

Coming from the trees at the edge of a grassy park were a line of mounted Natives, staying near the tree line and moving quietly. Jubal knew enough to stay under cover as Joshua came alongside. He pointed toward the trees, and they counted six warriors, leading two pack animals with fresh kills draped over the backs.

Jubal and Joshua were at the end of the trail near the tree line of black timber and at the crest of a ridge that revealed a grassy park showing itself to bend around a point of timber and stretch to the crest of the long ridge. The hunters were moving over the ridge and toward another park that lay in the basin between this ridge and another. Jubal could feel his heart beating, even hear it as he took only shallow breaths.

They had never been confronted with a band of Natives and knew nothing about them, what band they were, friendly or not, anything. They had been blinded by their lust for gold and had given no thought to the dangers of wandering around Indian territory. He had heard some talk of the Crow being friendly with the white man, and the Blackfoot having a treaty with the whites. But he had also heard of the way those that were at war with the soldiers and settlers treated those they fought with, mutilations, scalps, and more. His breath caught and almost choked him, but he fought the tendency to cough and make a noise. He had no idea what kind of sound would give them away or even how far the sound might travel in the timber. He glanced to the side to his brother and back to the small hunting party as they started into the thicker timber.

When the hunters disappeared into the trees, both brothers let out a long breath, not even realizing they had been holding it, looked at each other and grinned, chuckling quietly. "That was close. If I hadn't seen them, we'da been right out there in the open and no place to hide. No tellin' what woulda happened," declared Jubal. He stood, moved ahead, leading his horse and the pack mule, broke from the trees and stopped to look around.

Jubal pointed to what appeared to be the origin of the creek, "There might be some water there we can use. How 'bout we break a little ground, see what might be promising and wash a few pans. If we find somethin', good. But if not, I heard the waters of another creek back yonder, down in that other draw to our left. We can try there, maybe work our way across the mountains and see what we find."

Joshua sighed heavily, looked at his brother, and shrugged, "Good idea as any, I reckon."

The granite slabs showed lichen colors, but nothing that resembled a gold vein or any color other than the dusty grey of the high-country rock. While Josh checked the little pool of water where the spring slowly seeped from the rock face, Jubal used the pick to survey the rocks and rock formations. He drove the head of the pick into the ground, pulled up, and loosed some soil. He grabbed the pan nearby, scooped up the loosened soil, and started for the water. As he walked, he picked through the dirt, casting aside unpromising stones, and knelt at the water. He scooped up the pan full of water, washing the dirt around as he moved his fingers through the mud, tossed aside the dregs and scooped some more water. After washing the remaining portion, both men looked at the leavings in the bottom of the pan, but nothing showed gold. Jubal tossed the panful aside, washed out the pan and looked at his brother. "Nothing here looks promising. I've looked for any veins of off color, anything that looked like quartz, nothing but granite! I say we go on down to try that other creek, what say?"

"I'm game. Lead the way," replied Joshua, following his brother to the horses.

———

THEY PUSHED off the thick timbered crest and dropped into the narrow cut that carried the other creek. It was nothing more than a trickle and showed nothing different than the usual slide-rock shale granite that was prevalent everywhere. As they broke into a little clearing, Jubal looked to the sky off their left shoulder and the sun was beginning to dip into its palette of colors to decorate the western sky in brilliant oranges, golds and reds. He looked to his brother. "Let's look for a place to make camp, maybe a little further down the draw. It'll be dark soon and we need to make a decent camp if we wanna get any sleep tonight. What with the hunting party we saw, I don't want to have any fire showing after dark to give away our camp."

Joshua nodded, grunted and followed his brother. It was just a short way until the narrow defile bottomed out at the branch of another runoff creek. Jubal nodded toward the small clearing under a pair of big ponderosa that stretched high above the creek bed, and they began making their camp. Jubal stood, stretched, and looked about. He nodded toward a big rocky face that appeared to be nothing more than a massive boulder that slid down the mountain's face eons before, "I think I'd like to poke around that big rock face yonder, but not tonight. Maybe come morning I'll go over there and see what might be showing."

"You go right ahead. All I care about right now is getting a little fire going, get some and maybe cook up some of the pork belly and maybe some johnnycakes. Then I'm all for rollin' up in the blankets and get some good rest."

"Well," added Jubal, looking about, "we're in a low spot, shouldn't get much wind, and we're under some good cover. Maybe we will get a good night's sleep."

———

THE ANIMALS WERE PICKETED at the edge of the trees. The brothers had rolled out their blankets under the big ponderosa just above the little trickle of a creek. Jubal listened to the snoring of his brother, chuckled to himself and started to roll to his side, when the mule jerked at the picket line, his head held high, long ears pointing across the creek. The horses did the same and Jubal reached to his side and lifted his rifle, a Henry .44 caliber, and slowly jacked a round into the chamber, trying to be as quiet as possible. He held the rifle in his right hand and nudged his brother with his left. Joshua groaned, mumbled, as Jubal whispered, "Get your rifle. We've got comp'ny!"

Joshua rubbed his eyes, frowning, and looked to see Jubal sitting upright, rifle in hand, looking into the trees across the creek. Josh grabbed his Henry and rose to his knees, "What is it?" he whispered to his brother.

"Dunno. Maybe Indians, or…"

A flash of gray flitted through the trees, moving as quiet as the shadow it made until the mule cut loose with a bray that announced their presence to the entire mountainside. Jubal came to his feet, looking about as a blink of orange eyes caught his attention when a massive wolf lunged from the creekbank toward the horses. But the mule was on a long lead and stretched out his head, mouth wide open and snatched a mouthful of fur, flesh, and blood as the weight of the wolf drove against the big mule, but the mule stood his ground, shaking the wolf side to side as the canine whimpered and pawed at the air until the mule let go. The grey beast crumpled to the ground, a hunk of his throat still in the mouth of the mule. The pack animal spat the fur, looking to the creek for another attacker.

Jubal's Henry barked and spat fire into the dark of night, the lead finding its target of black fur that lunged from the thicket of willows that sided the creek. Jubal jacked another round just as Joshua fired his rifle. The flare of flame momentarily lit the night, showing a brief spot of grey fur, but the same beast lunged toward the mule only to be caught midair with both hind hooves of the mule who launched the wolf to a height among the branches of the pines that it would never have seen as it crashed through the branches before falling in a whimper to the ground.

The twins stood back-to-back, looking around their camp, their only light the last sliver of moon and the early rising stars, but they had grown used to the dark and searched the black for the even blacker shadows that revealed themselves by movement. Again, Jubal's Henry roared and spat fire, showing another black wolf with fangs showing, eyes glowing orange, but the bullet took its toll in the throat of the beast, driving it to its haunches as it snarled and spat blood before it choked to death.

The wolves had been attracted by the smell of meat cooking and after the twins had finished their meal, Joshua sat the greasy skillet aside, thinking to use it again come morning. But the smells of the cooking and that of animals was more than the wolfpack could resist and when darkness suited their purpose, they made their attack. Now the pack leader, his mate, and three others lay dead while two of the younger wolves of the pack had turned tail and disappeared into the trees.

As quiet fell on the camp, the boys began to relax and moved apart. Jubal looked at the first carcass, "We need to drag these away, or else we won't get any sleep at all, the horses will be spooked and the mule, well, he might tear things apart."

"I don't think I could sleep again anyway," mumbled Joshua. He rigged a sling for his rifle, hung it at his back, and grabbed one of the carcasses and started into the trees. Jubal did the same and they soon had the camp clear, although the smell of blood and wolf remained. Josh said, "How 'bout we stir up the coals and heat up the coffee?"

"I'm all for that. I'd rather the fire keep wolves and such away as to give away our location to any Indians," answered Jubal.

The small fire served its purpose and was quickly extinguished. The twins took turns snoozing and watching and morning did not come any too soon. Jubal nudged Joshua awake, "How 'bout you fixin' us some breakfast while I go check out that rock face yonder?"

Joshua rubbed his eyes, nodded, and came to his feet, "Look, Jubal, we've been out for over a week now. We've tried every creek on the east side of the Prickly Pear, and the most gold we've seen is the five flakes at the lower end of Warm Springs Creek." He shook his head, rose to his feet, the pan still in his hands as he pushed it toward the fire, "We've come to the headwaters of Prickly Pear and nothin'!"

"I know, I know. I thought we'd at least get somethin' up there. I was even hopeful we'd get something up that fork just up from Jefferson City, but nothin'." Jubal shook his head as he looked around, dropped onto a big granite boulder and sat, hands on knees as he looked around. "It seemed like a good idea at the time, you know, go upstream, pan till you find the source. But like everything else that seems logical, don't mean a thing. So, what do you think we oughta try next?"

"Everywhere we've been we've seen sign of others trying before us. We haven't tried any prospect holes, but neither one of us knows what to look for to start diggin'," shrugged Joshua.

"You fix breakfast," replied Jubal, "I'll try that spot over there and we can do others as we work our way outta the mountains. After that, what about trying Confederate Gulch? Those fellas we talked to before were pretty certain that was the place to go, maybe we shoulda followed what we thought before."

"Suits me. Go ahead on an' give that a try. I'll get the coffee goin'."

CHAPTER 27

LAKOTA

T*amiko Astsista-Mahkan*, Running Rabbit, was a leader of his people, long considered one of their most valiant war leaders, but the glint in his eye and the tug of the corners of his mouth spoke of his touch of mischievousness, yet there are those that see mischievousness when others see evil. He had a regal demeanor, broad shoulders showed underneath the beaded tunic, his loose hair that dangled over his shoulders sported three feathers stuck into a topknot, scalp locks adorned his tunic that hung over his breechcloth and buckskin leggings. Long fringe decorated with dyed rabbit fur trailed down the side of his leggings that over-hung beaded moccasins. He looked at Eli over the edge of his coffee cup, savoring the aroma and the taste of the white man's drink, "You are looking for your sons?"

Eli nodded, lowered his cup as he looked at his visitor, "Yes. Two sons, twins, that left their home at the time of the war back east. Their mother asked that I find them and bring them home."

"Will you do as she bids?"

"That's why I'm here, but my wife, their mother, has already crossed over and there is no reason for them to return home. But I made a covenant, a promise, to her before she died that I would find them and try to get them to go home. She was not a woman that knew the lure of these mountains and the way of a man that must see the new lands and more."

The chief nodded, sipped at his coffee, and said, "There are few women that know the will of man, and few men that know the way of women."

Eli chuckled, nodding, thinking of his wife and the times they had together, few though they were. His time in the army kept him away from her and her first husband, the father of the boys, had been killed before they were born. But he always thought of the boys as his sons. He looked at the chief, "They had joined the army to fight in the war but deserted and came west to get away from the fighting."

The chief frowned, looked long at Eli, discerning his intentions, "They are runaways, but you do not see them as weaklings? Do you believe they are brave enough to fight?"

"Can any man see his sons as cowards and weaklings? I know war, I was at Fort Laramie and fought the Lakota, the Cheyenne, the Arapaho, and the Absaroka. After Laramie, when the war began back east, I was transferred there, and fought in many battles, saw many die, and many other terrible things of war, and I saw those that turned and ran, tears on their faces, fear in their eyes, and yet the day before, they had fought valiantly, brave-ly." He paused, different thoughts racing through his mind, "Is it the man or the time that makes one a coward? Have you seen those of your people cut and run?"

"Yes. But among my people, if one does not stand and fight for his people, he is cast out in shame and driven away, never allowed to return."

"In a time of war, when a soldier runs away, he is considered to be a coward, he is tried and sentenced to death by firing squad."

The chief slowly nodded, looking at Eli, "Our people are much the same. Yet you seek those that have run away. Is it to take them back so they could be killed? Would it not be better to let them go? To live with what they have done may be worse than death."

"Do you speak as a father or a chief?" asked Eli.

"I speak as a chief; I question as a father." He looked at Eli, stretched out his hand with the cup and asked for more. Eli poured both their cups full, sat back and looked about. It was a fine day, the sky was a brilliant cobalt blue, no clouds marred the clear canvas of the heavens, and only a faint breeze whispered through the trees, carrying the slightly pungent smell of pines and the distant scent of elk, and further still, the sour smell of bear. It was the wilderness, and they were a part of the wild mountain land.

"Do you have sons?" asked Eli.

The chief nodded, "My women have given me three sons and two daughters. Only one son has grown old enough to seek the name of his manhood. Before they earn their final name, they are given one that," he paused, grinning and chuckling, "makes them want to earn a good name. My oldest son was called Little Rabbit by his mother, but the warriors gave him the name of Scared Mouse. He has gone with the others on a hunt, if he proves himself, they will give him a name as a warrior, as a man. Then, he can get him a woman and make his home to have children of his own, but that must be earned."

"Was he one of the hunters that took the elk?" asked Eli, remembering the band of hunters that killed some elk in the park.

"Yes. I saw him take the last elk. With one arrow, he killed the cow elk that will feed our people. He has earned a better name. Before the time of our treaties, our warriors could only get a man's name against an enemy. He could count coup, take horses, kill an enemy, or count coup against an enemy. But now, those names are earned as a hunter and provider for our people."

The two men sat silent for a while, savoring their coffee and their time together. Running Rabbit looked to Eli, "My village is camped near. Would you come with me to see my people and meet my woman?"

Eli lifted his eyes to the chief, began to answer, but the chief continued, "We will speak with the hunters to see if they have seen your sons. If they have not, they will look for them as they hunt in the days to come."

Eli nodded, grinned, "I would be honored to come to your village, to meet your family."

The chief let a smile split his face, the mischievousness showing, as he handed back the empty coffee cup. He looked at Eli, "I will get my horse and return."

Eli nodded, accepting the cup and snuffing out the remaining coals of the fire, wondering about the invitation, if it was in friendship or something else. As the chief rose to go, Eli stood and went to his horses to pack away the coffeepot and cups. As Eli tied down the pannier, he turned to see the chief returning, leading his horse, a tall black stallion with long mane and tail and a spirited step about him. The horse tossed his head as

Rusty turned to look and the two stallions looked at one another, nickering, lips moving and front feet prancing. Eli chuckled and stroked the head of his claybank, talking to him to settle him down. He kept a tight rein, stepped into the stirrup and swung aboard as Running Rabbit swung atop his black. The men chuckled, knowing what the stallions were thinking, but nudged their mounts from the trees, letting the chief take the lead, which did not sit well with Rusty, but Eli held him in check.

Rusty quickened his pace until he was beside the big black of the chief. Eli asked, "Are your people still bound by the treaty with the soldiers?"

The chief looked sidelong at Eli, "What we call the Lame Bull Treaty has my mark and has been honored by our people for this many," he held out both hands, all fingers extended to mean ten, "summers and more, but the white soldiers and the agents have *not* honored the treaty. They were to give much in what they call annuities and rations, but they have not done as agreed. My people were left to starve, but we have chosen to hunt. Now they come with another treaty. They want to take our lands, but we have not agreed, and their leaders have not agreed, but the white people still come, take the land, fight our people."

Eli knew of what Running Rabbit spoke, for it was often the case with the politicians in the Capitol, that they would protest the payments, appoint dishonest agents or expect the army to fulfill the obligations, and then they would come back later expecting the Native people to give even more. Eli had been at Fort Laramie when that treaty was negotiated and signed and had still been at Fort Laramie five years later when the treaty with the Blackfoot had been negotiated at the mouth of the Judith River and he had seen firsthand the contempt the leaders from Washington had shown to the Native peoples.

Eli shook his head, looked at Running Rabbit, "But not all white people are like that, just like all Native people are not like the renegades we both know that fight against the whites." He looked back at the chief, "The Lakota chief, Red Cloud, is making war with the whites now. The Sioux have been the enemies of the Blackfeet, are they still your enemies?"

"The treaty we have honored forbids us fight with those that have been our enemies. But the Lakota made raids against the Absaroka, the Piikani, the Gros Ventre, the Siksika, and more. If they come against us, we will fight and destroy them." The chief looked past Eli to the tree line about forty yards distant, his eyes flared, and he started to speak, but the whisper of an arrow passed Eli's head and as the chief ducked away from the arrow, the shaft buried its head in the shoulder of the chief. Running Rabbit slumped over the neck of his horse as Eli snatched his rifle from the scabbard and dropped to the ground, the big claybank stallion between him and the attackers. He slapped Rusty on the rump, dropped to the ground confident the stallion knew what to do. Eli was on one knee as he raised the Winchester to his shoulder, jacking a round into the chamber. Five Natives were charging toward them, screaming war cries and launching a flight of arrows. The Winchester bucked and a warrior jerked back, his feet rising beside the neck of his horse as he tumbled over the rump of the animal. Eli felt a tug at his shoulder, felt the burn of the arrow as it cut through his shirt and dug a furrow in the muscle beside his neck. But he had no time for that, the rifle roared again, and another attacker slipped off the side of his mount. The Winchester spat lead as fast as Eli could jack another round and drop the hammer. The barrage from the lone man shocked the attackers, three of their number already on the ground and bleeding out, another slumped over the neck of his horse, and the screams had silenced as the lone warrior swerved wide, grabbing the neck rein of the horse that still carried the wounded warrior and the two galloped into the trees.

Eli looked behind him to see the big black stallion, walking toward the trees, the chief with his hand twisted in the mane, his legs clinging tightly to the chest of the big horse. Eli stood, sounded the usual whistle that summoned Rusty. The big stallion trotted back, head lifted and tail flying, the grey followed close behind. Eli swung aboard, slapped the stallion on the rump with the flat of the stock of his rifle and quickly overtook the chief, "Running Rabbit, are you alright?" The arrow fluttered and quivered with every move of the chief as the man tried to sit upright. Eli said, "We need to break off that shaft. If your camp is not far, we can wait till we get there to take out the arrow."

Running Rabbit frowned, struggled to breathe, lifted his hand to point to the south, "There, follow stream through trees, camp there." He fell forward on the neck of his horse again, both hands twisted in the long mane.

Eli moved closer, leaned over the man, "I'm going to break off the shaft." As he reached for the arrow, Eli felt the warm flow of blood down his chest, but ignored the burn at his shoulder as he stretched out with both hands, his knee at the pommel of his saddle, and grabbed the shaft.

"Aa mato'tsit!"

CHAPTER 28

VILLAGE

"*Nikso´kowaiksi*, my friend," muttered the chief, trying to motion to Eli. Eli led the black horse of the chief behind his claybank as they entered the village of the people. Several warriors had come close, brandishing spears and bows, but the words of the chief stayed their hand as a woman grabbed the lead of the black and led the horse through the village. Eli followed close behind, the grey keeping pace. As they came to a clearing before several of the buffalo hide tipis, the woman hollered and motioned to others to help her get Running Rabbit down. Eli swung down and went to her side to help, and they soon had the man off the horse and into the lodge. She lay him on his stomach and began barking orders to several other women and a few men, prompting them to scatter as bidden. She glowered at Eli, motioned for him to leave, and spoke to another woman, motioning her to go with Eli.

When Eli stepped from the hide lodge, several of the villagers were gathered about and stepped aside as he started to his horses, but he was stopped by the voice of the woman behind him, "You are to stay with us. Running Rabbit would want that." The voice came in clear English, and he turned, only to see the back of a woman that motioned to him over her shoulder to follow her.

She was a tall woman, taller than most of the Piikani women, long hair glistened in the sunlight as it trailed loosely down her back. Her long buckskin tunic came just below her knees and she wore high-topped moccasins that showed beadwork on the sides beside the fringe. As she walked, she moved in the way of a confident woman, and she was all woman. Eli grinned as he watched her move, her figure filling out the tunic the way a woman should. She led him through the village, stopping in front of a lodge that was adorned with an impressive painting of hunters taking buffalo. She reached for the flap, pulled it back and turned to face Eli. She wore a stoic expression but motioned him into the lodge. He paused, looking from the woman to his horses and asked, "Shall I tether them near?"

"The boy will take them," she motioned to a young man that stood to the side watching the white man, "when you have taken your things."

Eli nodded and began stripping the gear and packs from the horses. As he dropped each item to the ground, the woman picked it up and carried it into the lodge. But when she reached for the saddle with the scabbarded rifles and heavy saddlebags, he said, "I'll take that."

She nodded, stepped to the entry, and held the flap for him as he stepped into the lodge with a glance over his shoulder to the young man who waited beside the horses. He dropped his saddle by the blankets and returned to the horses with a brush retrieved from the panniers. He gave the horses a rubdown and handed them off to the young man who led them away. Eli turned to see the woman preparing food for a pot that hung over a small cookfire. He said, "I am Eli or Elijah McCain. And you are?"

The woman nodded, "I am Morning Dove. Your food will be ready soon." She nodded to a willow backrest at the edge of a spread blanket, "You may rest there if you like. Do you have coffee you would like me to make for you?"

As Eli dropped to the ground, he winced at the soreness in his shoulder, felt the warm blood again as the wound opened up, but determined to attend to it later. He pulled the shoulder of his vest over the cut, and answered Morning Dove, "Yes, yes I do. I'll get it."

"I will get it. And you have a pot and cups?"

"In the panniers beside the saddle." He was not used to others digging through his things, but he did not want to do anything that might go against the way of the people that could cause offense. He sat back and made himself comfortable and relaxed. Morning Dove quickly returned—pot, cups, and coffee in hand. Eli watched as she filled the pot and put it near the fire, and as she tended the hanging pot of dinner, he watched, enjoying her way of moving and tending things. Every move seemed to be delicate, graceful, or rhythmic, almost as a dance. She glanced toward him and showed her first smile, but quickly turned her attention to her duties.

As he watched, he realized she was a beautiful woman, guessed her age in the early thirties, but he also noticed her coloring was a little lighter than the other Blackfeet, although her raven hair was just like the other women. He asked her, "Morning Dove, should you not be fixing the meal for your family instead of me?"

"My only family is Running Rabbit and his woman, Prairie Flower. She is my sister."

"Surely you have had a man of your own, haven't you?"

"I did have a man; he was killed by the Lakota. That was many summers ago."

"And this is your lodge?" asked Eli, motioning to the lodge behind him.

"Yes. I am also a warrior of the people and am also a healer. Among the people, it is the woman who owns the lodge and more."

Eli nodded, knowing that was the way with many of the Native peoples. "And you put my things in your lodge, is that for any special reason?"

"It is the way of my people. You have helped our chief and you are to be honored for what you have done. It is my duty to tend to your needs. You will stay in my lodge. I will take care of you."

Eli leaned back, wondering just how this was going to be, he was not one to take advantage of others, especially the women of the people. Although he knew they had different values and mores, but he had never been with another woman other than his wife and had no intention of changing his ways now. But she was a beautiful woman, nonetheless, he thought. Then he remembered the mischievous grin of Running Rabbit when he first invited him to come to the village. Maybe he was thinking of Morning Dove. Eli grinned and shook his head at the thought, *No matter where I go, someone is always wanting to marry me off to the first single woman they find. Why is it that folks just can't stand a man being happy alone?*

"If you're a healer, shouldn't you be tending to Running Rabbit?"

"His woman, my sister, is also a healer. She taught

me to be a healer. He has taken arrows before. He will be fine."

"You speak English very well, where did you learn?"

"There was a black robe who was called Father DeSmet. He taught many young people of the Kutenai, Piikani, Salish, and Siksika. There were other traders with our people, and I learned the language of the Métis, or French, the American Fur Company, and the language of other Native people—the Salish, Kutenai, Absaroka, and Lakota." As she spoke, she dished up a plate of the stew, poured a cup of coffee and took both to Eli. She dropped to her knees beside him, offered him the plate and cup and sat beside him. She smiled coyly at him, dropping her eyes, and speaking softly. "Do you not have a woman?"

"I did. She has crossed over."

"And did you have any children?"

"She had two boys, twins. That is why I am here in the mountains; I'm looking for them."

She frowned, "They are lost?"

Eli chuckled, "No, I don't think so. They left home some time ago and their mother asked me to find them and try to get them to go home to her."

Morning Dove frowned, "But you said she has crossed over."

"Yes, she has. But she asked that before she died, and I promised I would try my best to fulfill that promise."

Morning Dove lay her hand lightly on his knee, smiled at him, and said, "You are a good man."

He turned his attention to his meal, made quick work of it, and sat the plate on the ground and picked up the coffee cup, sipped on it, doing his best not to look at Morning Dove. He sighed heavily, gave a slight shake of his head, and thought, *This ain't gonna be easy*.

He sipped his coffee and looked up to see Prairie Flower walking toward them. She looked at her sister and then to Eli, "Running Rabbit wants you to come to my lodge. He wishes to talk with you."

Eli nodded, glanced from Prairie Flower to Morning Dove and sat his cup down to rise to his feet. He motioned to Prairie Flower to lead the way and he followed, with Morning Dove close behind. As he neared the lodge of Running Rabbit, Prairie Flower held the entry flap back and motioned him to go inside. He ducked through the opening and was surprised to see several other warriors seated around the central fire pit, although there was no fire burning. Running Rabbit was reclined on a pad of buffalo hides and was propped up into a semi-sitting position. He nodded to Eli, motioned for him to be seated at the foot of his blankets. As he was seated, Running Rabbit spoke, "I want you to tell the circle what happened. Morning Dove will translate your words."

Eli nodded and began, "Your chief and I shared some coffee and talked, when he invited me to come to your village…" he continued to tell of the unprovoked and unexpected attack. How Running Rabbit had taken an arrow and that Eli had helped him back to the village. When he finished, the others talked among themselves, anger and more showing on their faces and in their voices. One man spoke up, and in his own tongue, asked, "Running Rabbit said they were Lakota. How many were there?"

"Near as I could tell, five."

"You fought them?"

"Weren't much of a fight. I had a rifle, they had bows. I shot some, the others run off."

"How many did you kill?" growled the speaker, his anger and even hate showing in his manner.

When Morning Dove translated, she added, "You must be truthful."

Eli nodded, answered, "I killed three, wounded one, the other'n helped the wounded away."

"Why did you not kill them all? Were you afraid?"

"It would not be honorable for me to kill a wounded man or one that was leaving the fight."

"I do not believe this white man. He is like all the others, he lies!" snarled the speaker.

Eli noticed Morning Dove being hesitant to speak, but he encouraged her with a nod. When she finished, he glanced to the man, back to Morning Dove, "You tell him that he dishonors the lodge of his chief. I do not lie and if he says otherwise, we'll just have to take it outside." He looked at the warrior as he listened to the words of Morning Dove, and the man started to rise, but was shouted down by those around him and Running Rabbit growled, pointed to the entry, and told him to leave. Although Eli did not understand the exact words, he caught the intent in the manner and glanced around the circle. He looked at Running Rabbit, "I did not mean to dishonor your lodge, if I have, I will leave."

Running Rabbit shook his head, "It is Crazy Bear that has dishonored my lodge and my people. He is angry because you are in the lodge of Morning Dove. He has long wanted her for his woman, but she is a better warrior and hunter than Crazy Bear and he could not be her mate. For that, he has long been angry."

Eli shook his head, "I saw that look you had when you invited me here. Was it because of the woman, Morning Dove?"

The chief slowly grinned looking from Eli to Morning

Dove, and said, "She needs a good man. You are a great warrior. You killed three Lakota and wounded another in one fight. No other warrior can say such things. You would make a good mate; she would be a good woman."

Eli shook his head, grinning, and said, "I am not looking for a mate, but I am honored you would consider me to be a good mate for your woman's sister."

Running Rabbit chuckled, waved him off, and dismissed him to leave. Morning Dove led the way from the lodge, held the flap for him, and walked slightly behind him as he started toward her lodge. He stopped, looked at her, "You will have to walk before me or beside me. I don't know where your lodge is and I'm not comfortable for you walking behind me."

Dove smiled coyly, "Do you not trust me behind you?"

Eli chuckled, "From what I've seen of your family, none of you are to be trusted. Besides, when you walk behind me, all these," motioning to the other villagers that watched them, "will think you are my woman. Now, we don't want them thinking that, do we?"

Dove giggled, dropped her eyes and she stepped beside him and took his arm as they started to her lodge. She noticed Eli wince, frowned, and looked at his shoulder, pulling the vest aside. She looked at Eli, "You are wounded. You need me to tend to that. Come, now. I have my things in the lodge." She smiled as she pulled at his elbow, letting a slight giggle escape as her eyes flashed with the same mischievous glint he had seen in Running Rabbit's eyes. He shook his head and followed, grinning.

CHAPTER 29

QUARTZ

J ubal filled the coffeepot, returned to the campfire, sat it on the rock beside the flames, and looked to his brother, "I'm gonna take a look at the big rock yonder," pointing across the little creek and the rock outcropping that hung above the confluence of the two small creeks. Jubal had pointed it out when they first made camp, but the ruckus the night before with the wolf pack had taken it off his mind, but now he was focused and hopeful again.

They had been panning the streams and any rock formation that looked promising but had yet to find significant color. Jubal grabbed the pick, shovel, and a pan and started across the little creek, splashing through the shallows and pushing aside the willows. He crossed just below the confluence and started through the trees and up the steep slope. To his right, another large chunk of limestone seemed to teeter on another, but the colorful lichen and moss beckoned Jubal. As he moved closer, he saw nothing that would indicate anything but limestone or granite, but he dropped the shovel and pan, lifted the pick, and drove the head into the ground at the base of the boulder.

With the shovel, he stirred the soil, tossed aside some of the larger rocks and with the pan, he scooped up the loose dirt. He ran fingers through the dirt as he walked back to the water, lowered the pan into the water and with the current and his fingers, he filtered through the mud. Washing the pan around, letting the mud and silt spill out, he slowly allowed the motion to rinse through the remaining rocks and gravel. As he pushed them about, there was nothing that glittered, nothing that showed gold. He emptied the pan, rinsed it clean, and started back up the hill. As he passed the boulder, he grabbed the pick and shovel and moved higher.

The big outcropping appeared as one solid stone, a shelf of the stone had accumulated enough soil that a pair of scraggly piñon had taken root, claiming the shelf as their own. As he stood before the cliff face, he slowly looked over the rocky formation, the low sun of early morning still hiding behind the mountain, was leaving everything in shadows. But Jubal saw a variation in color that caught his attention, and he dropped the shovel and pan and stepped closer. At the lower edge of the cliff face was a vein of lighter-colored rock.

Jubal dropped to one knee beside the stone, reached out to the lichen-covered face, and below the grey of the limestone a different vein showed almost white. As his fingers touched the vein, he felt the crystal-like formation of the stone, and began to feel the entire vein which was about eight inches in width, but stretched across half the face of the cliff. He bent low to look closer, wiping dust and accumulated soil off the face, trying to see the vein unobstructed. A darker vein showed like a spider web across the face of the light rock, which Jubal was beginning to think was quartz.

As he fingered the darker vein, he began to get a little excited. Many times he had heard prospectors talk about the richest gold veins are usually found in quartz deposits. He moved closer, his face a few inches from the rock, his fingers tracing the darker vein and he saw something glitter. His eyes flared, his heart quickened, and his fingers touched and dug at the shiny spot. He grabbed the pick and slowly began digging at the vein with the head of the pick, gouging out a small portion, but his eagerness got the better of him and he stood, swung the pick back and struck the quartz just above the dark vein. Again and again he struck the quartz, trying to dislodge a piece that included the darker vein.

Small thumb-sized chunks fell, until another blow from the pick loosened a bigger palm-sized piece and another blow totally dislodged it, dropping it to the ground. Jubal dropped the pick, went to his knees and picked up the stone. As he brought it close to his face, his excitement split his face with a broad grin and he chuckled, then laughed. Shaking his head, he stood, lifted the pick again, and began striking the quartz with more excitement. He soon had a stack the size of a small campfire and he dropped to his knees again to sort through the pile.

He found other pieces that showed gold, and looked at the face of the quartz vein, shook his head, and stood, holding the two most promising pieces of stone, and started back to camp. He bounded down the face of the hill, splashed across the creek, and took the low rise to camp in three long strides. Joshua turned, frowning, "What's got into you?"

Jubal grinned, dropped the ore at Joshua's feet, and said, "Take a look!"

Joshua had been sitting on the end of a grey log, looked at Jubal and down at the rock. He picked one up, began turning it around as his eyes grew big. The sun was just climbing above the far mountain and now the light lanced through the trees and shone on the campsite. Joshua grinned and stood, looking from Jubal to the stone in his hand. "That's gold! We found it!"

Jubal chuckled as he saw the excitement on the face of his brother, but he held out a hand to stay Joshua's excitement, "Now, hold on a minute. Yes, that's gold, but it doesn't look like there's much in the vein. It's at the base of that big outcropping I spotted, and after chipping away, that's what I got. But...well, I'm not sure about it."

"Whaddaya mean? Not sure about it? That's gold, for sure and certain, that's gold," proclaimed Joshua as he pointed to the rock and held it out toward Jubal. "What's not to be certain about?"

"The size of the vein. It ain't much, but...well, let's eat and then we'll both go take a look. It was in the shadows when I was there, and by the time we eat, it'll be full light and we can see it better."

Joshua frowned, "But I wanna see it!"

"It ain't goin' anywhere, and if we're gonna be diggin' and such, we need all the strength and energy your breakfast can give us, so let's eat up!"

Joshua dropped the rock, bent to the frying pan and flipped the pork belly, shaking his head and mumbling all the while, with an occasional glance to his brother. Thoughts of riches and more were running through their heads as they tried to harness their excitement with their meal. But in short order, both men sat aside their tin pans, gulped their coffee, and were soon stomping their way back to the outcropping and cliff face.

Because it was a vein in the quartz, the only way it could be extracted was for the stone to be crushed and the gold washed out, but that was more than what they could do without the heavy equipment required. Their only means was to crush it with the pick or the sledge, sort out the bigger chunks, and wash the rest. They would still lose some that was deeply embedded, but they could get most of it, although it would be back breaking work. But the lure of gold and the promise of riches drove men to do more than they ever thought they were capable of or even had the means to accomplish.

The brothers soon had a system going. Jubal would swing the pick, loose the stones, and toss them to a pile on the shelf where the piñon held claim. But that was where Joshua would use the granite shelf where they cleared off the soil and crush the rock with the sledge. After they had a good accumulation of crushed ore, they would carry the ore in the emptied panniers down to creekside where it would be washed in the pans. The accumulated dust and nuggets were bagged in the leather drawstring pouches.

They worked as long as they had light, and even though they considered using the light of a fire, they were too exhausted to do anymore. But with the first light of morning, they had finished their breakfast and coffee, and were right back at the work. By late on the second day, it appeared they had exhausted the vein of quartz. Jubal crawled into the cut, trying to see the backside of the vein, but as he thought, the vein of quartz was finished, only little bits of quartz crystals and dust remained. He pulled back and stood looking at the face of the big stone that stood above him. The massive rock was the size of three freighter wagons and hung over the split that had been the quartz.

Joshua came from the ledge and stood beside his brother, "So, what do you see, or not."

Jubal shook his head, "There doesn't appear to be any more quartz, nothing white shows in there. But that doesn't mean the vein of gold is exhausted. It could be deeper and in between the layers of rock, but it'd be mighty hard to get at, unless we had some blasting powder." As they looked, trying to see every crack in the stone, the big boulder shifted just enough to groan and loosen some dirt and small rocks. The shift was not enough to be visible, but the noise and rocks told of the instability of the entire cliff face.

Both brothers jumped back when the stone shifted, each with a hand out to his brother, ready to run down the hill and away from what might happen. But there was no other movement, no more pebbles tumbled, no more groaning of the rock. The brothers breathed deep, not realizing they had been holding their breath, and visibly relaxed, looking at one another as a nervous grin showed on their faces.

"Ain't no amount of gold worth gettin' crushed to death," drawled Jubal as he bent to grab the pick.

Joshua responded, "Let's take what we can and get outta here 'fore it decides to slide down the mountain."

Jubal nodded, turned away as Joshua stepped up on the shelf to retrieve the sledge and shovel. He scooped up another shovel full, dropped it into the pannier and grabbed the leather strap, just as the big boulder shrugged and dropped another inch or two. Joshua jumped from the shelf, dragging the pannier behind him as Jubal shouted, "Move it!" and motioned for Joshua to follow him into the trees.

As they took to cover in the trees, the big boulder shrugged again, slipped a little, rocks and pebbles and dirt slipping, and with another big thud, the stone lost its footing and began to tumble down the hillside. It crashed into the trees, taking everything in its path, and within seconds, came to a stop at the confluence of the creeks.

Dust rose like a lazy cloud, drifting through the pines on its way up the hillside. The echoes of the thunderous roar of the rockslide bounced across the narrow valley and filtered themselves into silence. The brothers looked at one another, breathed deep and slowly moved from the trees. As they neared the site where the boulder had been, they looked all about, searching for any quartz or sign of more gold. The flat spot was littered with loose rock, shale, dirt and pebbles. Jubal walked across, kicking at the remains, seeing nothing promising, until a slight depression beckoned. He dropped to one knee, began pushing around the pebbles and soil, saw some promising glitter and turned to his brother. "Bring the shovel and the pans!"

Within moments, they had scooped two pans full and hurried to the creek. As they washed the pans, gold began to show, and the brothers' faces showed broad grins. When they finished with the soil from the little depression, they estimated they had washed eight to ten ounces of gold dust. They stood, looking at one another and laughing as they shook their heads. Jubal said, "Now that's what I call a profitable day's work!"

"Ain't it, though!" chuckled Joshua.

They knew there was nothing left in the depression and the creeks were already backing up, searching for a way past the boulder, so the brothers decided they would be safer and more comfortable back in town.

Joshua suggested, "We can wash out the rest of this downstream, and if we have enough, we can pay back our grubstake. Then…" he shrugged as he looked at his brother, grinning.

"Then we can decide what's next. I don't think this will be enough to last very long. But it's a good beginning. There's enough other places we can look, maybe add to the take, and soon have enough to leave the goldfields, maybe try the big city."

"I like the sound of that. The mountains are great, but I'm already gettin' tired of breaking my back. Say, maybe we could buy us a store or somethin', you know, a business to make us respectable members of the community, like Ma always said she wanted for us."

"You thinkin' about going back to Kentucky —see Ma?"

"Mebbe. We could at least visit."

"Yeah, maybe. But first, we need to take care of this, and maybe add a little to it."

CHAPTER 30

PROMISES

"So, just what is in that ointment you used on my wound?" asked Eli, watching Morning Dove as she bound the gouge on his shoulder with a pad of cloth under the strip of soft buckskin.

"It is a salve I make from the plant with a stem with four sides and a flower of purple lacy blooms, the root of the tall flower that grows after a fire and the leaves of the plant that bears big dark berries." She smiled as she tightened the strip of buckskin under his arm to hold the bandage tight on his shoulder.

Eli had pictured the descriptions of the plants, having a good knowledge of the many plants of the Rocky Mountains from his time at Fort Laramie, and thought the purple flower to be Bee Balm, the one that grows after a fire would be Fireweed, and the leaves from the Huckleberry. He grinned, "That's good to know. I might need to make my own sometime."

Morning Dove smiled, "But if you mix it wrong, it could kill you."

Eli chuckled, shook his head, "So, you're saying I should leave the healing to the healers?"

"Or," she smiled as she tied off the buckskin binding, pulling it extra tight to get his attention, "I could take you to where they grow, show you how to make the salve and other things," she grinned. "But it will take time together in the trees and other places." She stood, leaving Eli sitting on the buffalo robes as she looked down on him with a coy smile. "Running Rabbit would like you to stay with our people," she turned away and began arranging her sleeping pallet of blankets and buffalo robes.

Her pallet was well apart from his and he was relieved to see she would at least be on the far side of the fire ring, but she smiled as if the barrier was not a barrier at all. After arranging her blankets, she stood, looking boldly at Eli as she undid the tie of her tunic at the shoulder, which caused it to drop away and bare her shoulder. She reached for the other, and Eli quickly turned away, rolled to his side facing the wall of the lodge, although he heard her moving and was certain he heard a giggle. He closed his eyes and did his best to feign a lack of interest or concern.

The only light in the lodge had been from the small warming fire, the flames casting shadows on the hide covering, but now the flickering had faded, leaving glowing embers while a thin tendril of smoke danced its way to the open flaps at the peak of the tipi. Eli drifted off to sleep, comfortable underneath the heavy buffalo robe.

———

A SCRATCHING at the entry brought Eli instantly awake. The lodge was still dark, but the dim light of early dawn showed at the tipi flaps. He rolled over to face the entry, saw Morning Dove's blankets folded and sitting aside. He flipped the robe aside, stood and went to the entry, pulled the cover away and saw Running Rabbit standing, arms folded, and waiting. "Mornin', Chief. Come in, I'll be right with you."

He turned back to his blankets, found his boots, shook them out and pulled them on as the chief seated himself on the edge of Morning Dove's buffalo robe. He looked at Eli, "A hunting party returned after dark. I asked about your sons. The leader of the party, Buffalo Back Fat, told of two men, riding good horses, with a pack mule. He said they were stupid white men, made noise when they moved, talked loud," the chief dropped his eyes, shaking his head at the foolishness of the white men that know nothing of the way of his people and of the mountains.

"That might be them. Did your hunters say anything else about them, like how old, if they looked alike, anything?"

"All white men look alike," declared the chief. He let a slow grin paint his face as he looked at Eli, "Did Morning Dove please you?"

Eli chuckled, "Yes, she bound up my wound," he moved his shoulder to show it was good, "and she is a good cook. She asked me to stay so she could teach me the ways of a healer."

The chief smiled, nodding, "You will make her a good husband. Her lodge will never go hungry!" he declared, as if it was already done that they would be a pair.

Eli grinned, "Now hold on, hold on," he lifted his hands up, palms out, as he continued, "I said she invited me, I did not say I would stay. I gave my word that I would find my sons. *That* I must do before anything."

The chief's countenance sobered. He frowned as he looked at Eli, "Morning Dove will go with you?"

"No, no, no," declared Eli, shaking his head, "I'm not ready for another woman. Let me find my sons, fulfill my promise to my wife, and then, well, maybe..." he shrugged. He had no desire to take Morning Dove or to make any commitment to another woman or to the chief and his people, but he did not want to offend either the chief or Morning Dove. They had been gracious and kind, and he could not repay that with an offense, but he could not think of any other way to leave the village without offense.

The chief rose, looked at Eli, and motioned to the entry, "Morning Dove cooks a meal for us," and stepped through the entry. Eli stood and ducked through the entry, only to see not just Morning Dove, but the chief's woman and sister to Morning Dove, Prairie Flower, and three other women chattering as they puttered about fixing the meal for the chief and Eli. With a frown, Eli followed the chief to the two willow backrests that sat at the edge of the blankets and the two men seated themselves, accepting cups of steaming coffee as soon as they made themselves comfortable. Eli grinned, looked at Running Rabbit, "The only reason you want me to join with Morning Dove is so you can have a good supply of coffee," he chuckled and lifted the cup to his lips. The chief, doing his best to remain stoic and maintain his regal demeanor, hid his grin with his coffee cup, but his shoulders shook with his stifled laughter.

As they drank the coffee, Eli watched the women. Two were dropping hot rocks in a hole in the ground and quickly covering the hole with a sort of mat of woven sticks and leaves then covered it with dirt. Beside that hole, another one with a similar covering showed steam sneaking out around the edges of the covering. Morning Dove was attending a pan at the fire, but Eli could not see what she was doing exactly. And the meal was soon ready, and the women dished up two wooden platters full to hand to the men.

Eli was surprised when he saw two eggs, some camas root that resembled sweet potatoes, and another slice of something that reminded him of bread but he knew it was not bread. He frowned as he looked, sat the platter on his lap, and began peeling the eggs. Morning Dove sat beside him, her legs tucked under her as she leaned toward him, smiling. She saw his expression of consternation and began to explain, "The eggs are from ducks, they are steamed in the hole," she pointed to the holes that had been tended by the women. She pointed to the other items, "That is the root of the camas, and that is the back fat of the buffalo."

Eli looked at the items, frowning, and asked, "The back fat?"

"Yes. When it is taken, we cook it in oil, smoke it for three days, and it will last a long time. Our warriors take it when they go on a raid or a hunt. The white traders from the north called it Depuyer."

Eli nodded, having heard of Depuyer. He never hesitated to try new foods and readily began to enjoy the repast sat before him, but with almost every bite, he was reminded of the way of so many women, wives, mothers, sisters, friends and more, of the age-old custom of finding a mate for their only unattached friend, often resorting to joining with others to provide a well-prepared and tempting meal to entice the man to surrender. He chuckled as he enjoyed the eggs, the sweet camas roots, and the crispy-around-the-edges Depuyer that had a bit of a smoky yet sweet taste.

When he finished, he smiled, sat back and accepted another steaming cup of coffee from a smiling Morning Dove. She again sat beside him, leaning close and speaking softly, "When you are ready, I will take you on a walk to show you the plants I use for your bandage, and more, if you would like."

Eli took a deep breath that lifted his shoulders, glanced to a grinning Running Rabbit, and slowly shook his head as he enjoyed his coffee. He had to admit, she was a tempting prize, and she stirred feelings long forgotten, but he had a promise to keep, and he could allow nothing to keep him from fulfilling that covenant. He looked to the chief, "Did your hunters say how long ago, and where they saw the two white men?"

The chief nodded, reached for his coffee, and answered, "It was two suns ago, north of here about a half day's ride. He said the two men had camped near the joining of two creeks."

Eli knew if they were two days ahead of him, the only thing that would slow their progress would be for them to strike gold and he was skeptical of that happening. With the many other gold hunters and experienced prospectors, he doubted if there were any rich deposits unclaimed, but he also knew that stranger things had happened. He looked to Morning Dove, "How 'bout we take that walk now?" She smiled and rose to her feet, offering her hand for him, and with a nod and a smile to her sister and the chief, she took Eli's hand in hers and started toward the trees.

CHAPTER 31

PURSUIT

"Why have you not taken a man as your husband? You are a beautiful woman, respected by your people, and there are many men in your village, surely you have had those that would want to share your lodge," asked Eli, as the two walked together along the banks of the small creek. Morning Dove had led the way to the place where the different herbs and plants used by the healer could be found. She had pointed out the tall shaft of the Bee Balm with the purple flowers and the pink blossoms of the fireweed.

When Eli asked the question, she paused, turned to look at him and answered, "There have been those that have sought me as a wife, but Crazy Bear was determined that he would allow no others to have me." She paused as she looked about the little clearing, started toward a patch of flowers, "These are the yellow lily, or glacier lily. We make a hot drink with the leaves when someone is sick, here," pointing to her belly. "Many women use it to keep from being with child," she smiled as she dropped her eyes.

Eli continued his inquiry, "But Crazy Bear doesn't look to be that great a warrior, so why would not someone else challenge him?"

Morning Dove grinned, "I am a greater warrior than Crazy Bear. I have counted coup, stolen the horse of a Sioux chief from his lodge, killed warriors in battle. I have taken buffalo, elk, deer, and the bighorn in the high mountains, but I have not killed a bear. Many of the other warriors are…" she struggled for the words and Eli interjected, "afraid?" She frowned, "They believe they would be shamed to be less than their woman. Crazy Bear only wants to be with me because he thinks that will make him greater in the eyes of other warriors." She looked at Eli, "The man who was my husband was a great warrior and a war leader. He was respected and honored by the other warriors, but not because he was my man, but because he was a great warrior and hunter. Crazy Bear does not understand that. I could not be with Crazy Bear, even if he was a great chief. I do not respect him," she chuckled, "he smells too."

Eli grinned, understanding. He looked to Morning Dove, "I am attracted to you, and I respect you. I would not be intimidated or afraid to be with you, but I have given my word to the woman who was my wife, that I would find our two sons. I must do that before I consider any other direction for my life."

They started back toward the camp and Eli added, "The woman who was my wife was a good woman, but we did not have much time together. I was always away from home with the army. I was at Fort Laramie for several years, then the war came, and I fought in the war back east. We did not have much of a life together, but I married her because she had been the wife of a good friend who was killed. He had asked me to take care of his wife, who was due to give birth. I agreed." They walked in silence for a short distance and Eli stopped, turned Morning Dove to face him, "I have often thought of a woman that would not just stay at home and cook, but a woman to walk beside me, go with me when I travel or journey to distant places. You are such a woman. I would like to come back after I finish my search. Would that please you?"

Morning Dove smiled, leaned into Eli and hugged him. She leaned back, looking at Eli, and said, "You are the only man that I have known that would make me proud to be your woman. Yes, I will wait for you." They embraced again and walked together back to the village. Their smiles and laughter told the villagers much and generated much talk, especially among the women. When they returned to the lodge, they ducked inside and Eli began searching through one of the panniers and came out with a buckskin-wrapped bundle. He stood before Morning Dove and held it out to her, "You said you never killed a bear. Take a look at that."

She looked up at him, timidly accepted the bundle, and began to unwrap the buckskin. As it opened, her eyes flared and she looked up at him, wide-eyed and back to the package. She gingerly took one of the items out, held it close and looked at it. The long claw of a grizzly bear was longer than her fingers, and she looked at the rest of the bundle and back to Eli. "You took a bear, the great bear of the mountains?"

Eli grinned, "Didn't have much choice. He was mauling a man and had to be put down. Took all I had to do it, and he come after me, scared me, too, but I finally dropped him." He nodded to the bundle, "Cut them off cuz I knew they were used by Natives to make necklaces and such, thought they might be good trading stock, but I want you to have them. Maybe you could make something special."

She dropped the bundle by her sleeping pallet and moved closer to Eli, tears in her eyes, and embraced him, holding him tightly for several moments. When she finally loosened her hold, she leaned back, and said, "You are a great warrior and a great hunter. I am proud of my man." She turned away before he could respond and picked up the bundle again. As she fingered the claws, she spoke softly, "I will make a band of the claws, beads, and hairpipe. It will be the envy of every warrior and every woman."

"Could you make one for each of us, matching?" asked Eli, smiling.

Morning Dove smiled broadly, "Yes, I will do that."

He had explained to her earlier that he would leave the village to resume his search and she had sent the boy for his horses. The young man scratched at the entry to tell of his arrival and Eli flipped open the entry cover, nodded to the young man, and accepted the leads of the horses. After ground tying them beside the lodge, he fetched his saddle as Morning Dove carried out most of the panniers and bundles. He was soon geared up and ready to go, but his reluctance showed on his face and Morning Dove drew near, took his hands, and placed them at her waist as she leaned into him for an embrace.

As they pulled apart, Eli held her hands for a moment, dropped them and reached for the saddle horn as he stepped into the stirrup and swung aboard the big stallion. He looked down at Morning Dove, smiled, nodded, and nudged Rusty to a walk that drew the lead of the grey taut and he rode from the village.

As he rode away from the village, Eli did not look back. He was surprised he felt as he did, heavy and somewhat sad at leaving Morning Dove. It had only been a little more than a day, but the time spent with her stirred thoughts he thought he had locked away, never to be revived. He shook his head, trying to clear his mind, focusing his thoughts on his search for the twins. Running Rabbit had said to go north following the creek that turned west away from the trail. Then to cross the flat, over a bench and find the trail of the white men with their pack mule. It was little enough to go on, but he was certain it was the twins that had been seen by the hunting party. He would have liked to talk to the hunters, but Running Rabbit had sent them out on another hunt to the southeast mountains.

Early afternoon saw Eli crossing the flat above the headwaters of Prickly Pear Creek. This was the park that the group of hunters with Running Rabbit's son had taken the elk. Although the offal usually attracted an assortment of carrion eaters, the gut piles had been devoured and nothing showed except a few ravens and magpies. He pushed Rusty to take to the saddle crossing that split the timber-covered bench. A well-used game trail marked the way, and they soon approached another grassy park. Eli reined up at the tree line and reached back to his saddlebags for the binoculars. He had learned long ago of the peril of putting yourself in the open without knowing what was waiting.

As he scanned the park, the only movement was a fox on the hunt and a rabbit that appeared to be taunting him, playing with him, but nothing else moved but the tall grasses in the raggedy afternoon breeze. But Eli had that crawling-up-his-back-uncomfortable feeling that something was wrong, or waiting—something that threatened him. He watched, searching the tree line across the park, but still nothing. He swung down, moved to a big ponderosa that stood at the edge of the trees, and used it for cover. Leaning against the rough-barked tree, he scanned the park and surrounding tree line, but again, nothing. He glanced back at Rusty who stood, head high, ears pricked and nostrils flaring. The claybank stallion bobbed his head, snorted, and backed up a couple steps, preferring the trees to the park.

Eli looked back at the park, saw movement at the upper end and watched as a big boar silver-tipped grizzly ambled into the open, stood up on his hind legs, and sniffed at the air. He dropped to all fours and took off at a run, the big ruff at his front shoulders rolling with each lunging step of the big bruin, as the beast charged toward the near side of the park. Eli followed the bear with his glasses, stepped away from the tree to see where he went, and watched as the boar gave chase to a cow elk, trailing a gangly calf. Within a few bounds, the grizzly barreled into the calf, knocking it tumbling, and whirled to sink his teeth in the neck of the pale brown bellering calf. The big bear took the calf down, breaking its neck as he fell, and stood astraddle of the carcass as the big cow stopped at the edge of the trees and turned to see the massive bear as he tore into the dead calf with his long claws and teeth. The cow watched for a moment, dropped her head and turned away and disappeared into the trees.

Eli mounted the skittish big stallion, grabbed the lead for the grey packhorse and moved out. He stayed with the trees and rode around the big park at the west end, turned back to the north to find the game trail he spotted before, and started up the slope that he hoped would take him to the west-flowing creeks where his sons had been seen.

It was about an hour later as he neared the crest of the long timber-covered ridge, when the game trail he followed, crossed another and it was on that trail he spotted the tracks of two shod horses and a mule. He grinned, looking at the trail, and was certain these were the tracks of the boys' horses. He nudged the claybank onto the trail as he leaned down for a better look. He judged the sign to be at least a day, probably two or more days old. But protected as the tracks were on the trail in the trees, he was hopeful he would soon find where they had been or maybe even where they were still.

CHAPTER 32

HOPE

Eli was well experienced at reading trail sign, schooled by the Crow scout Half Yellow Face when he was stationed at Fort Laramie. He remembered the words of his friend, "Let the sign speak to you. They have much to tell you, but you must look, listen, and learn." Eli chuckled at the remembrance and how often he had stumbled over things that spoke loudly to Half Yellow Face, who would often mock him for his failures.

Eli looked at the sign below, stepped off Rusty, and went to one knee beside the trail. He touched the tracks, looking at the differences, noting the tracks of the mule that were narrower than the typical horse, seeing the depth of the tracks that told of riders and packs. The mule was not heavily loaded but was carrying packs, and the riders stopped often, usually where there was a clearing or nearby stream that might suggest the possibility of gold.

Whenever there was a rock formation near a stream, he saw the sign that told of the riders stopping and washing a few pans of soil, told by the imprint of a heavy pan, an empty pan, and footprints behind the imprint of knees in the soft soil, then continuing on their way. Eli glanced off his left shoulder to the lowering sun, looked ahead on the descending trail, and thought the bottom of the descent might be the place to make camp.

The trail he followed kept to the west bank of the little creek; the east bank showed a long talus slope of grey slide-rock. It was less than a quarter hour when the point of the ridge to his right ended at what might be the confluence of the two small streams told about by the hunters. Rusty paused, lifted his head, and Eli spotted the small clearing that showed all the sign of a camp. He nudged the big stallion into the clearing, stopped and looked about. He could see where they had spread their blankets, built their fire and dragged heavy panniers back from the creek bottom.

He stepped down, looked around and decided to make camp and take the time to try to read the sign and get an idea what the twins were doing. He stripped the gear from the horses, stacked it under the wide branches of a ponderosa, let the horses roll and rubbed them down with the brush and picketed them within reach of the scant grass and near the water. He had spotted the big rockslide carried by the massive boulder and was anxious to look the site over before the light faded.

It was obvious where they washed the pans just above the confluence on the creek fork nearest the rock-slide. Both men had busied themselves with the pans, but they had to get the ore from somewhere. Eli stood, splashed across the little creek and stood, hands on hips as he looked at the site of the rockslide. Powdered quartz remained on the bit of a shelf that now showed split trunks of the two piñon trees that had clung tenaciously to the cracks of the shelf, but the big boulder had made splinters of them. He saw the signs of digging in the soil that had been under the big rock and the sign told the story of the short stay of the brothers. Eli made one more look, walked around the area, and returned to his camp.

As he built his little cookfire and prepared his coffee and meal, he thought about the twins and what they were probably doing with the results of their diggings. He hoped they were not bent on splurging on a big time in town like many men are after a long absence from home, but they were young and Eli hoped not so foolish. He knew Madame Beauchamp at the Red Rooster had given them a grubstake and if they chose to repay her, the temptations of the flesh might be a greater temptation than they could resist. But that's all he was doing, guessing at the possibilities of the behavior of two young men that he did not really know.

And that thought brought back the memories of his years away from the home of his wife and family. So many times he had wanted to go back to the farm and be with the family, but duty always interfered and he had been taught to stand up to his responsibilities as a man and the responsibility of his oath and uniform always managed to take priority over family. Because of the family's fortunes on his wife's side, he had always been assured they were well provided for, even if his officer's pay was minimal in comparison, but nothing, no amount of wealth or possessions could take the place of the presence of a father. And even though the boys were not his natural offspring, they were his sons nonetheless and he also had a responsibility to his family.

As he watched the pork belly sizzle in the pan, he shook his head at his failures, but also realized it was impossible to change the past, but if he could find the twins, talk to them, maybe convince them to return home…perhaps their lives could become a testament to the goodness of his wife and her family if not his own. He had to find them.

————

JUBAL AND JOSHUA rode the trail from the rockslide following the little stream down the cut between the long heavily timbered ridges. When the creek bottomed out, it bent to the north and converged with another slightly larger creek that pushed its way through the willow-lined banks. Jubal reined up, looking around and turned to Joshua, "We've been up here before. This is the first creek we followed up. This is Warm Springs Creek," he chuckled, stood in his stirrups and pointed to his right and into the valley, "it's right up there where it forks again. I'm thinkin' they called that the north fork and the middle fork of Warm Springs Creek." He chuckled again, looked at his brother, "You remember that don'tchu?"

"Yeah, I remember we didn't see as much as a flake of gold anywhere on that whole creek!"

"Yeah, but right down here at the confluence would be a good place to make camp and finish washin' the rest of the ore. There's some big rocks there we can use to break it up 'fore we wash the pans, and we can get a better idea how much we got 'fore we go into town."

It was just past midday and the sun was high in the cobalt blue and cloudless sky. They found a spot in a bend of the creek where a couple cottonwoods sided the willows and alders and offered a good sandy bank at the creek. They stripped the horses and mule, tossed their bedrolls beside the cottonwoods, rubbed down the horses, picketed them in the shade at a patch of grass, and eagerly went to work to finish washing the ore and sorting the dust and nuggets.

When dusk was dropping its curtain on the setting sun, the twins stood, hands at their hips and arched their aching backs but grinning at one another. Jubal said, "I'm guessing we got maybe twenty ounces, what'chu think?"

Joshua squinted, looking at the pouches of dust and nuggets, "I think those two bags of dust will top ten, twelve ounces each. And that bag of nuggets, another ten."

Jubal grinned, shaking his head, "Feels good, don't it?"

Joshua nodded, grabbed up the three bags, and started to their bedrolls. He called over his shoulder to his older brother, "Bring the pans and such, I'll stash these!" Jubal stared after his brother, shook his head and chuckled as he picked up the pans, the pick, and the sledge. Jubal traded the gear for the Dutch oven, frying pan, and coffeepot and went to the fire ring where Joshua was laying in a fire. Joshua looked at his brother, at the oven and pan, and asked, "What'chu fixin'?"

"That's what I was gonna ask you!" declared Jubal.

Joshua grinned, "Uhuh, it's your turn. I fixed it last night and this morning. It's this cook's day off!" he chuckled as he sat back from the little flames licking at the stacked wood. He grabbed the coffeepot, and said, "I'll fix the coffee, but only cuz yours ain't worth drinkin'!"

Jubal rose and went to the packs for the cornmeal, flour, sugar, and the smoked meat. He remembered seeing some onions and camas roots he would add to the stew. He whipped up some cornbread, put it in the

Dutch oven, and set it beside the fire. Using the shovel, he drug some hot coals away from the fire, sat the oven on top, scooped up some more and put it on the lid. Satisfied, he went to work on the stew just as Joshua took the lid off the coffeepot that sat beside the fire and steam rose from the hot water. He scooped up the ground coffee beans from the rock, dumped them in the water and replaced the lid.

Satisfied with themselves, the boys sat back to wait for supper. Jubal leaned back against the big cottonwood log, locked his fingers behind his head, and looked at his brother. "So, you thinkin' about what we're gonna do after we cash in?"

Joshua sat on a big rock, elbows on knees and looked at his brother, "A lot depends on how much we have after we pay back Madame Beauchamp, but yeah, I've been thinkin' about it. How 'bout'chu? What'chu thinkin'?"

"Well, part of me says we oughta have a celebration, you know, like some o' them fellas do at the tavern and such, but you know me'n liquor don't get along too well, so…" he shrugged.

Joshua looked sidelong at his brother, "I've been thinkin' 'bout them neighbor girls back home. You know the two redheads, what was their names?"

Jubal chuckled, "What's their name? You know as well as I do, what's their name. I heard you talk about 'em so much; you even did it in your sleep!" He shook his head and mocked his brother with a squeaky voice, "Oh Elizabeth, Oh Eleanor, you girls are so pretty!" he laughed as Joshua picked up a stick and chucked it at him.

Joshua shook his head, "I always thought it'd be somethin' for twins to end up with twins."

"Well, they were pretty, that's a fact. But with what

we done, deserted and all, I don't think their pappy would be too receptive of us as sons-in-laws."

They dropped into a moment of reflection and memory until Jubal asked again, "So, if we don't have enough to go back home, what do you think we oughta do?"

"There's always Confederate Gulch, or we could even go down Virginia City way, or..." He shrugged, glancing to his brother.

Jubal sat up, went to the fire to stir the stew and check on the cornbread. Joshua sat back, looking a little pensive, lifted his eyes to Jubal, "I wasn't going to tell you, cuz I was keepin' it back as an emergency fund, but Gran'ma stashed away a sock of gold coin in the bottom of our saddlebags."

"She did what?" asked Jubal, frowning at his brother.

Joshua nodded, "Yup. I didn't find it till we were packin' the panniers. Surprised me too. But I reckon that's what she had in mind, you know, money just in case we had an emergency."

"How much?"

"Bout five hundred in gold coin."

"Five hundred dollars?! And you weren't gonna tell me?! I oughta wring your neck!" growled Jubal, frowning at his brother.

As Eli rode into Montana City, he spotted Mama's and remembered the good food and meeting Madame Beauchamp. He nudged Rusty to the hitchrail, slapped the rein around the rail, grabbed the lead of the grey and did the same. He stepped up to the boardwalk and pushed through the door that rang a little bell at the top edge of the doorjamb. Eli stopped, looked around and spotted an empty table near the window and seated himself.

He had no sooner taken his seat than he was greeted by Marylou who recognized him right off. "Well, if it isn't Mister McCain." She chuckled, "I see that Margaret didn't catch you in her web the other day. So, what'll you have, sir?" she asked as she poured the cup full of coffee. Eli frowned, looked at Marylou, "Maybe somethin' sweet, what'chu got?"

She smiled, "Well, other'n me, we have Spider Cake and some Apple pie."

"Spider Cake?" asked Eli, frowning.

"Ummhmm, it's peach cobbler in a cast-iron skillet. Folks like it right well."

"I'll have some of that, please."

"Comin' right up!" she declared and turned in a flounce and smiled back at him over her shoulder as she headed to the kitchen.

Eli chuckled as she walked away, turned to look out the window, and heard a woman's voice, "Did you find them?"

He turned to see Madame Beauchamp sitting at a table sipping on a cup of tea that she held before her. She was dressed conservatively and modestly, her reticule dangling from her left wrist as she looked askance to Eli.

"Not yet. I've been on their trail, but haven't caught up with them yet."

"They were here two days ago. Paid me back the grubstake and a little to boot, so I did well."

Eli leaned on the table, looking toward the woman, "Did they say…" but before he could finish she inter-rupted with her hand held before her, then motioned for him to join her. He rose and went to her table, slid out a chair opposite her and sat down.

She nodded, and began, "I asked them if they had seen you, and of course they said no, and were surprised

I knew you. When I inquired as to their plans, they were a little evasive. Joshua said they were thinking about returning to Kentucky, a couple of neighbor girls were on his mind. But Jubal did not look too interested in Kentucky and asked what I might have heard about other strikes. I told him about Confederate Gulch and Diamond City, and a couple of other strikes around. It seems that those stories get started every time one prospector finds a nugget and they think it's the mother lode!"

"Nothing else?"

"No, but I was impressed they didn't 'tie one on' and blow what they did have. The assayer, he's a regular at the Rooster, said he paid them off for a little over thirty ounces. But that's not enough to really do anything with. The girls said they had talked about getting enough of a stake to buy a business of some kind, become 'respectable gentlemen.'"

Eli frowned at her use of 'the girls' but he understood. He did like the thought of them buying a business, but their mother's family already had a very profitable business raising horses and tobacco. Yet he also understood wanting to make it on their own. But now, where would he go? If they returned to Kentucky, all the better, but he could not let go the thought that they would be looking for a bigger strike, a better stake, enough to fulfill their dreams. He fully understood the dreams of making it on your own, that was why he went to West Point and started a career in the army. That was his dream then, but the war changed a lot, not just for him, but for the twins.

He walked from the café, looked around the town, decided to make a camp nearby and take some time to decide where and how to further his search. He glanced heavenward, muttered a short prayer, *Lord, I need your help. I don't know where they went, where they are, or how I'm gonna find 'em. But, you and I both know the promise I made to their mother won't be fulfilled until I do. So, help me, please.*

He sighed heavily, grabbed the reins of his big stallion, swung aboard and leaned down to grab the lead of the grey. He sat upright, looked around the one-street town, and said, "Alright Rusty, you decide." The claybank turned his head back to look at Eli, lifted his head, and moved his lips, as if to say, "Wherever I go, you go, so hang on!" and with that, the red dun stretched out and moved as if determined to put civilization far behind. At least until his rider got some sense...

A Look at: Escape to Exile
Stonecroft Saga Book One

AUTHOR OF THE BEST-SELLING BUCKSKIN CHRONICLES SERIES TAKES US ON AN EPIC JOURNEY IN THE NEW STONECROFT SAGA

It started as a brother defending the honor of his only sister, but it led to a bloody duel and a young man of a prominent family lying dead in the dirt…

Gabriel Stonecroft along with his life-long friend, Ezra, the son of the pastor of the African Methodist Episcopal church, at his side, the journey to the far wilderness of the west would begin. One man from prominent social standing, the other with a life of practical experience, are soon joined in life building adventures.

That journey would be fraught with danger, excitement, and adventure as they face bounty hunters, renegade Shawnee and Delaware Indians, and river pirates. The odds are stacked against the two young men that were lacking in worldly wisdom when it came to life on the frontier. But that reservoir of experience would soon be overflowing with first-hand involvement in happenings that even young dreamers could never imagine.

AVAILABLE NOW

About the Author

Born and raised in Colorado into a family of ranchers and cowboys, **B.N. Rundell** is the youngest of seven sons. Juggling bull riding, skiing, and high school, graduation was a launching pad for a hitch in the Army Paratroopers. After the army, he finished his college education in Springfield, MO, and together with his wife and growing family, entered the ministry as a Baptist preacher.

Together, B.N. and Dawn raised four girls that are now married and have made them proud grandparents. With many years as a successful pastor and educator, he retired from the ministry and followed in the footsteps of his entrepreneurial father and started a successful insurance agency, which is now in the hands of his trusted nephew. He has also been a successful audiobook narrator and has recorded many books for several award-winning authors. Now finally realizing his life-long dream, B.N. has turned his efforts to writing a variety of books, from children's picture books and young adult adventure books, to the historical fiction and western genres which are his first love.

Printed in Great Britain
by Amazon

26311088R00142